THE PAST & THE PRESENT

THE PAST & THE PRESENT

KAYT C. PECK

SAPPHIRE BOOKS

SALINAS, CALIFORNIA

Editor - Heather Flournoy
Book Design - LJ Reynolds
Cover Design - Fineline Cover Design

Sapphire Books Publishing, LLC
P.O. Box 8142
Salinas, CA 93912
www.sapphirebooks.com

Printed in the United States of America
First Edition – November 2019

This and other Sapphire Books titles can be found at
www.sapphirebooks.com

Dedication

To the kids next door. Your sweet spirits and inquiring minds give me hope for the future and remind me why it is that I am called to write.

Acknowledgments

To Mary Emeny, John Scott Campbell, Nancy Bennett, Cyndy Walton, Sylvia Renick and to many others who encouraged me through a dark but productive time. Thanks also to Mary Rose Henssler and James Phelps, both of whom I trust to tell me the truth with kindness. As always to Chris and Schileen and the crew at Sapphire Books. I am so honored and proud to be one of your authors.

Prologue

The flames of the campfire licked and flirted with the rays of moonlight as a fingernail moon peek-a-booed through the Ponderosa pines. The three companions rested in companionable silence. For many minutes, the crackle of the fire and the occasional hoot of an owl were the only sounds.

"What happened next?" a girlish voice asked from the darkness just beyond the circle of firelight.

"You've heard this tale a thousand times," Kidwell Brown answered with a soft chuckle. She ran her fingers through her brown hair now flecked with hints of gray. The slight stiffness of the hair from the sweat of the day's exertions gave her an odd sense of pleasure.

"And I want to hear it again," the voice answered.

"The drug lord's minions had taken me totally by surprise, and I was captured in my own kitchen, knowing that nothing short of a miracle could save me," Kidwell said.

"They came for you because they knew you were the one who had taken the drug lord to prison," the young voice added.

"Who is telling this story?" Kidwell asked.

"You are, Auntie," the girlish voice answered. She spoke out of courtesy. Normally, the young female transferred her thoughts directly from mind to mind, as was the custom among her kind.

"There's a chill this night," the third companion interrupted with a heavy Gaelic accent, ancient in its intonations. Her long, auburn hair was still neatly contained in a single tight braid running down her back. The sword leaning against a log added to her anachronistic presence. She moved closer to Kidwell and opened her cloak, letting in the chill night air for an instant before she pulled Kidwell close, wrapping them both in its ample folds.

Kidwell smiled, as always, touched and a little disconcerted at Maolan's protectiveness. She wasn't accustomed to being protected.

"And here is the miracle who saved me," she said, snuggling closer to the warrior. "I had no clue she was there until I saw a bronze-tipped arrow erupt through the chest of the man who was about to shoot me."

"I knew naught if I could do it, come to this world through a portal," Maolan said. "But I had to try."

"But the men, the…?" The girlish voice from the darkness paused, not remembering the words.

"The FBI and the State Police," Kidwell said.

"Yes, them. They had been warned."

Kidwell felt Maolan stiffen beside her. "Aye. We couldn't reach Harrana," Maolan said, using Kidwell's ancient name. "But your mother thought of a way to warn the sheriffs of this land."

"Mother's never told me. How did she do that?" the young voice asked, sounding mystified.

Maolan stiffened yet more, and Kidwell held tightly to Maolan's hand. She turned slightly, looking into the face of her protector.

"We need to tell her, my dear. She will only keep asking." Kidwell cleared her throat and continued. "There is another here who knows Maolan from the olden days, one who could hear and see her through a portal."

There was a slight gasp of surprise from the darkness, more of a rumble than a gasp. "Annalome?" the young voice asked.

"Aye," Maolan said bitterly. "The woman whose weakness betrayed us all in ancient days. The one whose failure doomed your uncle, Falong, to death in battle and this world to millennia of darkness." She held Kidwell tighter, leaning in to touch her cheek against Kidwell's as Kidwell placed an arm around Maolan's waist. "The one who doomed me to be separated from the only one left whom I loved so dearly, your sweet auntie here."

Kidwell felt hot tears fill her eyes. It still pained her to think of Anna, the woman with whom she had shared so many lives. She did not have Maolan's release of hate. Despite a more recent betrayal, Kidwell could not hate Anna. She missed her still, despite waking in the night, reliving that moment when she came home to find Anna had succumbed to weakness, to the comfort of another, a woman whose beautiful face hid a darkened heart.

"But...but Annalome helped you when you became a Prophet?" the child asked.

"Yes, she did," Kidwell answered. "Her heart is good, child. It is faith in her own courage she lacks."

Maolan pulled away slightly, but Kidwell held tightly. "Finally, we are together, Maolan. Let's not think on what might have been but enjoy what is." Kidwell spoke quickly, striving to change the subject. "Those were adventurous times, too, when both Aisha and I were called as Prophets."

"White Buffalo Calf Woman came to you at the

kiva in the cave," the child said, excited.

"Yes," Kidwell answered. "And Kadijah came to Aisha in a vandalized mosque."

"And you had to hide beside a sacred, hidden lake when your prophecies came true and bad people wanted to kill you?"

"Yes, but we survived, and more and more people are seeking to find their own answers, to focus on healing and love," Kidwell answered. She yawned deeply. "And now, sweet niece, it's time you went home."

Kidwell reluctantly left the warm cocoon of the cloak and Maolan's arms. She walked to her tent and retrieved her pack, carefully pulling a piece of rough wood wrapped in a soft towel from a bag hanging on the side of the pack. As she unwrapped the wood— an elongated piece, cut from a knot in a large tree—a painting appeared of a large eye, so real it seemed to move in the moonlight.

In the darkness, a young dragon stood from where she had lain talking with her companions. She was a shadowy outline in the darkness, but Kidwell admired the magnificence of her dragon niece.

"Do I have to?" the young dragon whined in answer.

"I promised your mother you could only stay long enough to keep us company for the evening." Kidwell stepped nearer the fire and raised the painting, one of the first magical creations of Aisha, her co-Prophet and an artist whose paintings were portals between worlds. "Now, Allana, give your mother my love, and go home to your own weyr."

"When will you come back?" Allana asked.

"My work is here for now," Kidwell answered. There was a part of her who longed to return through the portal with her niece. For 10,000 years she had been separated from her dragon existence, reincarnated as a human lifetime after lifetime and living with the woman who had once been her rider before the defeat of the great battle.

Allana turned to Maolan. "Are you coming with me?"

While Kidwell was dragon become human, Maolan was a human who had become dragon in the aftermath of the war, when magic separated the worlds and protected others from the corruption that had entered human Earth. Now, both had the power to choose between their dragon and human forms. After spending millennia as a dragon in the dragon world oblivious to any human technological evolution, Maolan lived as a major anachronism now that she could walk again in the human world.

Maolan smiled. "Not this night, child." She turned to Kidwell. "I wish to stay here for a night."

The painting had come to life and was looking at the young dragon. "Allana, it's time to come home," a voice came through the painting.

"You heard your mother," Kidwell said.

"Oh, all right. Love you, Auntie. Love you, Maolan."

"Love you, too," the two women chorused.

The young dragon transformed, becoming smoke or mist or liquid, and the huge creature flowed toward the eye and through. When she was completely gone, Kidwell carefully wrapped the painting and put it safely back in its bag.

"I'm tired," Kidwell said. "It was a long hike today."

"You could have flown," Maolan said. Kidwell

had been able to master transforming into dragon in either world.

"It's not safe to be dragon too often. For now, it must remain a secret."

"Aye," Maolan answered. She opened her cloak again and wrapped it around them both. They kissed gently. "I wish to lie beside ye this night."

"And I wish to be beside you," Kidwell answered.

They entered Kidwell's tent, ignoring the sleeping bag Kidwell had carried with her on the hike. Instead, they huddled together between the warm furs Maolan had brought with her through the portal. What they enjoyed that night was simple comfort in the presence of the only beings in the universe with whom they each felt totally safe.

Chapter One

Unexpected Guests

The headlights made two overlapping circles on the garage door as Greg pulled their SUV into the driveway. Weariness slowed his responses, and he took a deep breath before reaching up to the sun visor and hitting the button that would open the automatic garage door. In the passenger seat, Aisha awoke at the mechanical sound of the rising door. She rubbed at her eyes with the heels of her hands.

"Finally, we're home," she said.

"Can't wait to sleep in our own bed," her husband answered.

Aisha reached across the console and placed her hand on Greg's thigh. "What would I do without you?"

Greg barked a laugh and then drove slowly into the garage. "Not get any sleep on the drive back from Santa Fe."

"That among other things," she responded. "The paintings are selling well, amazingly, all over the world. I am so grateful that you are with me on these tedious journeys doing the business side of my art."

Greg put the transmission into park and turned off the ignition. As Aisha reached for her door handle, he placed a hand on her shoulder, causing her to pause and turn to look at him.

"Are you ever worried, well, that people don't

know what they're buying?"

"You mean that they have no idea they are magical portals?"

"Yes," he said.

"All the time. But I learned long ago to simply do what I know I must do and not worry about what I cannot control."

"Sometimes I envy you. The guides come to you. You know things others cannot, and you have faith, real faith."

Aisha leaned across and kissed her husband on the cheek. "And you have faith in me. I am grateful for that more than anything else in the universe."

"How could I not?" Greg said. "I was there when we met Kidwell and Anna. I know what happened to you and Kidwell. I'm not a fool. The gods called you both. I can only stand in awe."

Aisha laughed. "Right now, you can stand in awe all you want, but I'm going to lie in our bed and sleep just as soon as my head hits the pillow. Let's leave the bags in the car. We can get them tomorrow."

"Sounds good to me."

As they existed the SUV, Greg stopped at the door between the garage and the house, holding it open for his wife. Aisha stepped just inside the door and froze.

"What's wrong?" Greg asked.

"The light is on in the kitchen," she whispered. "And listen."

Greg stepped beside her and they both stood meticulously still, focused on listening. A distinct rumble of purring could be heard.

"We don't have a cat," Aisha said.

Greg glanced askance at his wife. "You think? What kind of burglar brings a cat?"

Aisha closed her eyes and stood, her face reflecting more deep listening, but Greg knew his wife well enough to know she wasn't listening with her ears. As she focused, Greg looked around the garage, finally taking a short-handled shovel from where it hung on the wall. He raised it as a weapon and stepped in front of his wife.

"It doesn't feel evil," she said.

Cautiously, Greg stepped into the house, the shovel raised above his head, ready to strike a blow. He jumped abruptly around the corner and into the kitchen, poised for a fight. Instead, he gasped in surprise at the incongruous sight before him. Aisha stood on her tiptoes and looked over his shoulder. In an instant, a deep belly laugh erupted from the diminutive woman.

Sitting casually at the kitchen table were four figures. The purring stopped abruptly as two feline humanoids looked up in surprise at the new arrivals. Between them rested a carton of Rocky Road ice cream, and each feline held a long-handled spoon. Flecks of ice cream were visible on the fur and whiskers around their mouths. Also at the table were two stereotypical angels, white robes and furled wings included. Between them was an open jar of dill pickles, and the angels' faces were contorted into puckered, sour expressions.

"It took you long enough to get here," one of the felines said.

Greg recognized both cat people from the first of the portal paintings his wife had created, driven by obsessive visions. They had delivered many paintings to the Santa Fe gallery, but Greg and Aisha kept that first painting. It felt like it would always belong to them. Greg had assumed it was because it was the first, and because of the striking beauty of the feline man and woman, perfect in physique and dressed in armor of leather and mail, the man with a sword strapped to his back and the woman holding a bow with a quiver of arrows hanging from her side.

"We had paintings to deliver," Aisha answered. She stepped around her husband, who still stood with mouth gaping, shovel at the ready. Aisha took the shovel from her husband and leaned it against the doorjamb. She put a hand on each hip and scowled at her unexpected guests. "I see you've made yourselves at home."

Both angels placed their half-eaten pickles on the table and wiped their fingers on their pristine white robes. No stains appeared.

"Please forgive us," one angel said, his face losing its pucker. "We don't get to take corporeal form often, and neither of us had tasted sour before."

Greg shook his head, regaining his composure. "I think we have some SweeTARTS left from the Halloween candy we bought for the neighborhood kids. Want to try them?"

"Oh, yes, please," the woman angel said.

"Angela!" the other angel said. "Our friends are home now. We must focus on our mission."

Greg laughed. "I don't think a little candy will distract you too much." He crossed to a cabinet and rummaged for a mostly empty bag of miscellaneous candy, all of the caramels and chocolates already gone, leaving only a few SweeTARTS and licorice in mini packets. He placed the bag on the table, and both angels greedily grabbed at the candy.

Aisha stepped close to the table and looked inside the nearly empty ice cream carton. "And you two?" she asked, looking pointedly at the felines.

The male cat-man took a spoonful of some of the last of the ice cream, purring as he placed it in his mouth. The cat-woman sighed and put her spoon on the table.

"We became bored and went exploring," she said. "When we opened the magical cold box there"—she pointed to the refrigerator—"this smelled so delicious, we decided to try it."

"We couldn't stop," the cat-man said, wiping at the ice cream on his face with the back of his hand and then licking at the fur. The gesture was so reminiscent of a cat grooming itself that it gave Greg a momentary feeling of vertigo.

"You better finish it before he does." Aisha picked up the spoon and put it in the cat-woman's hand. The cat-woman rapidly complied, the male glaring at her as she scooped up then licked at the last of the ice cream, her own purr accenting her obvious pleasure.

The male angel stood. "Please, let us introduce ourselves. I am Nathanial, and my companion is Angela." He gestured to the felines. "This is Morris and Lala."

"Morris? You're kidding," Greg said.

Morris sighed. "My parents found a portal that viewed into a human home, and they enjoyed the plays on the magic box, especially the short tales of feline feasts."

Aisha looked at Greg, and chuckled. "Cat food commercials."

Greg smiled at their guests. He hesitated for a minute, wiping his hand on his shirt before offering it to the angel for a handshake. The angel shook Greg's hand heartily. "I'm Greg and this is—"

"We know who you are," Nathanial said. "You are why we are here."

"Then you must be here with a message for my wife."

Nathanial gestured to his companion. "Yes, we are here to meet with Aisha."

The male feline arose from his chair. He stood nearly seven feet tall.

"And we're here to welcome you, my friend." The cat-man clapped Greg on the shoulder in a violently friendly gesture.

"You both look weary," Angela observed. She stood, crossing to Aisha. After placing her hands gently on Aisha's shoulders, she leaned close, touching the woman forehead to forehead. Greg heard his wife gasp softly with pleasure before Angela moved to him, repeating the friendly embrace. As soon as their foreheads touched, he felt enlivened, younger even, and involuntarily replicated his wife's gasp of pleasure.

Morris reached for the sword and scabbard leaning against the kitchen wall. Lala moved to retrieve her bow and quiver from where she'd left them beside a cabinet.

"Come, Greg. We have much to teach you.

"Come where?" Greg asked.

"To our world," Morris answered. "We are to train you for war."

Aisha gasped. "Greg, I..."

"Don't worry," Lala said. "We will keep him safe, and, for now, it will only be for a few days."

"And we have much to discuss in his absence," Nathanial said to Aisha.

Feeling excited and fearful, Greg followed the two felines toward the studio where their painting rested.

He paused as he walked past his wife. Spontaneously, they held each other in an intense embrace, exchanging the kind of lovers' kiss only possible when facing an unknown future. The two angels smiled softly at the sight, but the cat-man laughed.

"Come on, man. This is no permanent parting We'll only take you for a short time, a few days at most, at least this time."

Greg turned to his wife, his eyes asking what he did not feel comfortable saying. She knew him well enough to see the question in his eyes. *Should I trust them?*

Aisha closed her eyes. As he watched, Greg knew that she had opened that part of her mind and heart that listened and heard the messages intended only for a Prophet. Greg was aware that she waited to hear, as she so often had before, what she had described to him as a whisper in Kadijah's familiar voice. The first and most trusted wife of the Prophet Mohammed had been her primary guide from the first vision that had launched her into life as a modern Prophet. Greg watched his wife's face and knew she'd received her answer.

"Yes, darling husband. You can trust them," Aisha said.

Greg gave his wife's hand one last squeeze and followed the felines, secretly thrilled at the coming adventure. When they arrived at the studio, he saw that the cherished painting only included the odd-colored trees and grass of a different world. The figures central to the painting were, instead, standing alive and real in the studio. As Lala stood before the painting, she morphed into a stream of steam or mist or liquid, flowing into the portal, followed by her male companion. When Greg's turn came, he was frightened yet excited at the sensations he suddenly felt.

So, this is what Kidwell meant when she said it felt like being drunk, he thought as his very being took on a liquid form. It was odd feeling like water in a glass.

❧ ❧ ❧ ❧

Nathanial and Angela sat at the table, two cups of black coffee before them. Angela sipped at the hot, dark liquid.

"This is not sour, but it's similar," she said.

"It's called 'bitter,'" Aisha answered.

"Is it sometimes?" Nathanial asked.

"Always. That is why many people use cream and sugar."

"He does not mean the coffee," Angela said. "He asks about you being called as a Prophet."

Aisha looked long into her own cup, a lighter brown from the cream and sugar she had added. "Sometimes, yes. There are moments I miss the simpler times when I did not feel the weight of the world on my shoulders. When my greatest concern was grading student papers and finding galleries for my paintings."

"And the responsibility of great magic?" Angela asked. "How does that rest with you?"

"The paintings make me feel more like a conduit than an artist. I pray they have meaning."

"They do," Nathanial said. "Great change comes, and it could not be possible without the portals you create."

"Change can be good or bad," Aisha said.

"And we must all work together to strive for the good," Angela said.

"We know that you must feel alone sometimes. You were called as the healer and Kidwell as the protector, but the time is coming when neither of you will be alone in those roles."

"What do you mean?"

"Today, we are only here to give you hope and comfort and to assure you that you are not alone. If you find yourself in darkness, know that the light comes," Nathanial said.

"What do you mean?" Aisha asked again.

"That is all we can give you today," Angela responded.

A sound of music, pleasant but without melody and uncertain as to whether it was voices or instruments, filled the room. Both angels looked to one another, then each took a long, savory drink of the bitter coffee.

"We must go now," Nathanial said. "Know that you are never truly alone, without comfort or protection."

Aisha watched as they simply faded from solid to light and the light flew away, passing through the ceiling as though it were not there. Aisha carried the cups to the sink, wondering as she did so when her husband would return.

Chapter Two

Monster Hunt

Kidwell was home. She'd hiked alone back from her rendezvous with Maolan and Allana, but the lone walk had been no hardship. In some ways she needed that time to transition, to feel that she could truly belong in the human world, one that had been her home for lifetime after lifetime. Living two entirely separate existences was confusing at best. Sometimes it felt as though Kidwell died as she transformed into her ancient self, the once forgotten existence as Harrana, a dragon, part of two dragon-rider pairs that once served as the protective vanguard for both worlds. They had failed, and for many centuries she'd been spared the painful memory of that failure. Even when it returned, she could not feel, as Maolan did, that Annalome's weakness was the sole cause. Kidwell, then Harrana, had been dragon and Annalome the rider. If there was not the strength to complete the magic they'd been given, it was a failure they shared. A demon horde had found its way to the human world, but Annalome had not the strength to hold the magic staff that closed the portal. Only a partial victory ensued. Those demons already here had stayed, but in ethereal form, able to act only through influencing humans weak or black of heart.

As she hiked that day, alone with her thoughts

and only slightly comforted by the warmth of the sun and the smell of pine trees, Kidwell wished for the return of the amnesia that had blocked the memory of that battle. Her adopted brother, the grand dragon Falong, had died protecting them as Annalome and Harrana wielded magic. His rider Maolan had never lost the grief of his passing. There was no bond in the universe like that between dragon and rider.

With their failure, the veil between worlds closed, protecting others from the contamination of human earth. Maolan became dragon, choosing that world and returning Falong's body to his home. Kidwell became human, choosing that world, staying to share human lives with the woman who had been her rider. With Falong's death and Annalome's failure, the Four were now Two, and Kidwell took great comfort in sharing a new life with Maolan.

Arriving back at her home, a small ranch nestled in the Rocky Mountains, for a time Kidwell was able to simply enjoy the life she'd made there. Martin, the young Apache who was her self-appointed guardian, greeted her as she stepped out of the tree line and crossed the county road that ran beside the house and barns.

"Did you see them?" Martin asked.

"Yes, as planned," Kidwell said.

"Maolan still bitchy?" Martin asked.

Kidwell laughed. "I thought you liked her."

"I do. I'm just a little worried about accidentally pissing her off," he responded. He met Kidwell several yards from the house and matched pace with her. "Something about that sword she has strapped to her back, I guess."

"They just don't make shield maidens like that

these days."

Martin's face turned grim. "Glad there was an old-time shield maiden around when you needed her."

Kidwell glanced at the young Apache, a man whom she loved like a son. She knew he was regretting a time when he wasn't there to protect her. Only the unexpected arrival of Maolan through a portal had saved her from execution at the hands of a drug baron's minion. Kidwell stepped closer and punched the young man not too gently on the arm.

"Hey! It's okay, *hito*. I'm still here, still alive. Even if I wasn't, it wouldn't have been your fault, you big goof. You can't be everywhere."

"Yeah, well, I just hope you don't go on any more stupid missions."

The air was filled with a powerful silence.

"You won't promise that, will you?"

"Martin, there are things I can do that no one else can."

"That's why it's so important that we keep you around. Kidwell, you and Aisha are *The Prophets*. You have bigger fish to fry than catching a few bad guys."

"Martin, that drug lord I nabbed and who is being tried by the World Court, his whole operation has fallen apart. I hear from the Mother Superior who first asked for my help that the people in her village no longer live in fear. That little escapade of mine saved hundreds, maybe thousands of lives."

He grasped her arm and stopped in his tracks, turning Kidwell to face him. "We don't need a martyr, Kid. We need you. The spirits talk to you. They give us hope, and they can only do it through you. Don't throw that away."

Kidwell could face a demon without blinking,

but she stared at the toes of her boots, unable to bear the pain she saw in her soul-son's eyes.

"I'll think about it," she said.

Martin sighed shakily. "Think fast. An FBI agent delivered a package for you today. It's from Roberto at the World Court."

                  ⋙⋙

The young Apache paced the kitchen, his long black hair flowing in the self-made breeze each time he made a rapid about-face. His friend, his mentor, his soul-mother sat calmly at the table sipping at her coffee and intently studying an official brown file folder. Kidwell focused most on the photo of a distinguished-looking man in an expensive suit as he prepared to climb inside a black limousine. The pages accompanying the photo belied any appearance of normalcy implied by the picture. His financial success came at the price of hundreds of thousands of lives.

"You can't go again," the young man demanded. "The last time you were nearly killed." He pulled a chair harshly from the table, pointing emphatically at the empty chair. "In this very chair, in this kitchen!"

"Actually," the woman responded, pointing at another chair beside the table. "I think it was that chair. I moved them around when I was cleaning last week."

"Aye, aye," the young man exclaimed, striking his forehead with his palm. "The exact chair does not matter. It has only been a few months since we purged this home of the spirits of the men who died here, those who came to take your life but lost their own."

Kidwell's hands formed into fists where they rested on the table. His words had found a weak point in her armor of peacefulness.

"I did not wish for them to die," she said.

Martin sat in the chair he'd pulled from the table and moved it abruptly so that he sat near Kidwell. "And I do not wish for you to die," he said. A tear drifted from his left eye and down his cheek. "I was not here to protect you. I failed you."

Kidwell placed her hand over Martin's where it rested on the table. "Oh, Martin, you've never failed me. We had no clue that the drug lord's followers would realize I was the one who captured him, who imprisoned him."

She rose from the table and retrieved the coffee carafe from where it warmed in the coffee maker, then refilled both their cups where they rested on the table. The movement gave the proud young Apache a moment to discreetly wipe the tear from his cheek. Kidwell knew well this young warrior, her self-appointed protector. She wished to preserve his dignity. He had been with her nearly from the beginning. He had been the first to greet her and her companions when they found their way to the sacred Tewa Thunder Lake. She and Anna were refugees from factions within their own government, those who wished to punish Kidwell for the accuracy of her prophecies, and Aisha and Greg were refugees from radical Islamic groups that were angry at the accuracy of Aisha's prophecies. The spirits themselves appointed Martin their guardian, and he never flinched in his service. Over time, love held him to that service more than any sense of obligation, As Kidwell looked at the strong young man, she felt a pride and love as intense as any woman had ever felt for a son. Kidwell placed a gentle hand on his head for a moment before taking her place back at the table.

"Martin, you have saved me in so many ways. I trust you more than anyone else in the world, but you cannot always protect me."

"If it is in my power, I always will," Martin answered. He jabbed a finger at the file folder on the table. "Even if it is by persuading you from your own foolishness."

Kidwell leaned back in her chair and sighed. "Martin, do you remember what I said about my days in the Navy and then as a firefighter?"

Martin laughed. "I remember many things you have said about those days. Which one?"

"That sometimes you have to do dangerous things as safely as possible."

"Yes."

Kidwell looked intently at the young man. "I can do things no one else can do. You know that, Martin."

"And does that mean that you must always be the one to be put at risk?"

"Many times, yes," she answered. "Especially in a case like this."

"What do you mean?"

Kidwell swiveled the folder so that it was directly in front of Martin. "This man is a monster. Harold Swinford is his name. He was Army special forces in the early days of the war in Afghanistan. After leaving the Army, he formed a security and arms business and, for many years, was a primary contractor to the US government, providing mercenaries and arms to hot spots all over the world."

"A man with dirty hands in a dirty world, but how does that make him a monster?"

"He enjoys the killing, the subjugation of people." Kidwell reclaimed the folder and rifled through the pages. "His contracts included developing and staffing incarceration facilities for prisoners of war, until reports could no longer be denied that those were largely fronts for the trafficking of women to the sex trades and the selling of arms to the highest bidder, including those whom the US fought. He's in exile now, a guest of those who are most definitely not allies of the US, or much of anyone else for that matter."

Kidwell lifted a page, reading, until she turned away in disgust. "Those incarcerated, many at his whim, were also subject to his personal, shall we say, pleasures? He's a sadistic bastard."

"There are many such monsters in this world. Why does this one merit risking your life?"

Kidwell leaned close. "You know the secured call I made to Roberto after I opened the package?"

"Yes."

"Martin, I cannot tell even you what he told me, but know that stopping this man is important to save the lives of huge numbers of people."

"Weapons of mass destruction?" Martin asked.

"With the desire, the means, and key partners to use them," Kidwell answered.

Martin closed his eyes, and his face contorted in pain. "Mother of my heart." He opened his eyes, staring intently at her face. "Do dangerous things as safely as possible."

As though on cue, the laptop resting on the table erupted into a telephone ring. Kidwell touched the keyboard and the face of a dark-skinned Mayan dressed in a business suit appeared on the screen.

"*Hola*, Roberto," Kidwell said. Despite the circumstances, she smiled at the representative of the World Court, her partner in the capture and trial of monsters.

"Are you willing to do this?" he asked, almost breathless.

"Of course."

Relief was apparent on Roberto's face. "I am sorry to ask this of you my friend, but if we do not act quickly..."

"I understand, Roberto."

"Our source says that he is alone in his room now, most likely fast asleep."

"Then it is time to act," Kidwell said.

"*Vaya con dios, mi amiga.* If all goes well, I will see you here at The Hague in a few moments."

"I shall see you soon," Kidwell said, cutting the connection to the call. Kidwell pulled a page from the folder, a detailed photo of a bedroom, opulent and ornate in furniture, bedding, and the art in the oversized room. She studied it, memorizing as much detail as possible.

She stood and crossed to the roomiest part of the kitchen. She closed her eyes and spread her hands in front of her. A flow of color sucked the woman inside. Then it coalesced into something new, deep black highlighted in flashes of rainbow. Kidwell was gone, and Harrana the ancient dragon stood in her place.

"I don't know if I'll ever get used to that," Martin said.

Harrana chuffed in dragon laughter, a puff of smoke drifting from her nostrils. She raised a clawed hand in salute, then she was simply gone.

"No, I'm not going to get used to that," Martin said to the empty kitchen.

≈≈≈≈≈

Harrana morphed directly to the room depicted in the image she held so closely in her mind. With practice, her skills were improving. She was one of the only two remaining of the ancient species of Eastern dragons, born as much of magic as of flesh, products of the very early times. Flight without wings had been the earliest of the old skills she remembered, but she was getting better at teleportation, size and density manipulation, and even invisibility. There was barely an instant after reforming in Swinford's bedroom before the iridescent black dragon became invisible to the physical eye.

She paused, unmoving, silently getting her bearings. With great relief she heard a loud snore coming from the bed, and she moved cautiously in that direction. She stood over the sprawled man sleeping soundly in disheveled bedclothes. She noticed hints of fresh blood on the sheets, and she wondered with disgust if she had been too late to prevent the man's initiation of yet another young girl.

That ends now, she thought. She gently placed one clawed hand on the man's bare shoulder while envisioning yet another room half a world away, one with bars for one wall, and Roberto and two trusted, uniformed guards awaiting her arrival. So gentle was the transition that the sleeping man barely stirred as she transported him from his opulent bed to a narrow bunk with starched white sheets and a one thin synthetic blanket.

A snore died mid-breath as the man threw his arm over his eyes, blocking them from the harsh light.

"What the Hell?" he yelled as the two guards descended upon him, holding his arms and legs.

Again Harrana was instantly invisible, but her friend Roberto, a World Court prosecutor, grasped toward where he knew she must be. When his hands made contact, he began pushing her toward the open cell door. Normally, the man could not have budged the dragon, but she moved willingly.

"Get out!" he whispered harshly.

As soon as they were both out of the cell, Roberto slid the door closed behind them with a loud clang. Then he led the way down the corridor, out of sight of the cell. When they were in a darker corner, Harrana looked around, still invisible to the physical eye. She glanced up at a security camera hanging above.

"I know you're there," Roberto said. "Go home. We'll talk later."

But do you need me here? Harrana willed the thought to be heard by her friend.

"No, I want you to go. That is the mistake we made before, keeping you here. That is how you were seen and identified."

There was the momentary flash of black and rainbow as Harrana teleported. When she re-appeared in her own kitchen, she converted immediately to her human form. Martin looked up from where he sat at the table, astonishment reflected in his face and posture.

"But, you just left," he said.

"Easy, peesy," Kidwell answered.

"Did you…?"

"He was in a cell and being subdued and searched as I left."

Martin's laugh spoke more of relief than humor. "Then you're safe."

"Safe and hungry," Kidwell answered. "Interested in an omelet for a late lunch?"

Martin stood and moved toward the counter. "I'll fix lunch." Martin pointed with his lips, Apache fashion, toward the hallway and the stairs on the other side. "You'd better go let them know you're safe or Maolan may suddenly appear threatening to roast us both."

Kidwell laughed. "Right you are, and she could do it, you know."

"But she won't." He pulled an onion from the cupboard and paused to smile at Kidwell, his own relief at her safe arrival reflected in his eyes. "She loves you."

Chapter Three

Unfinished Business

Masat, Harrana's adopted sister, using her gift for manipulation of the portals, had enlarged the eye-shaped window within her daughter's chamber in the family caverns of the weyr. All three dragons gathered around the image of Kidwell as they spoke through the dragon eye portal, the one that, in the human world, hung in Kidwell's bedroom.

Maolan fidgeted nervously. The depth of her emotion heightened the color of the emerald scales on her chest where they were warmed by her heart.

"You should take me with you on these captures," she demanded, not for the first time.

"Maolan, we've been over this. I've not mastered teleportation enough to take another with me. Besides, my world is not yet ready to welcome an ancient warrior maiden from pre-history."

"Was he awful? You have such adventures," the young Allana asked eagerly.

Kidwell smiled gently at her adopted niece. "Yes, child. He was awful, or they would not have asked me to go for him."

"What did he do?" the child asked.

"Allana," bellowed the deep maroon dragon who was her mother. "This is not a story from long ago. It is real, and not a tale for your entertainment."

Kidwell looked at her niece with sad eyes. "She is right, Allana. I would not tell you the things he has done. I pray you never have to know of such things."

Maolan visibly relaxed. "You are safe now, and in your home."

The emerald dragon and Kidwell exchanged a look, a wordless communication. Maolan would make use of a portal later that night, one that would carry her human form to Kidwell's side. Masat turned her face away, hiding the smile that showed she had seen and understood the private message.

"My dears, I must go," Kidwell said. "Martin is fixing a meal, and I am very hungry,"

"Go, dear sister," Masat said. "And thank you for letting us know so quickly that you are safe."

The portal darkened, shrinking in size and looking most like a pool of flowing mercury contained in the shape of an eye on the cavern wall.

"May I go to tell Leeon of Harrana's latest feat?" Allana asked her mother.

"Yes," Masat answered. "I am pleased you two have become such great friends, but be back before the full dark of night."

"I will, Mother," Allana said before leaving through the open exterior doorway and launching herself into flight from the cliff outside.

"She is a good child," Maolan said. "Do not be too harsh on her. She is proud of Harrana and all she does in the human world."

"I do fear sometimes," the mother said. "Allana still sees adventure but does not understand the pain and danger."

The maroon dragon curled into a comfortable position, settling in for a long and peaceful conversation without her daughter's interruptions. The emerald dragon did the same, pulling her legs beneath her, looking for all the world like a huge cat comfortably settled into the "meatloaf" position.

"And what of you, old friend?" Masat asked. "I cannot imagine your confusion taking human form again, walking in the human world."

"And reuniting with one of the Four," Maolan said.

"When Harrana first came through the portal, seeing my lost sister after so many millennia filled my heart with joy, but I felt lost, like my world would never be the same," Masat said. "I cannot imagine what it's like for you. You Four were the vanguard, the hope of dragonkind and humanity alike."

"The four of us, we shared a love and a bond that, well, went beyond time. I have never stopped grieving what we lost, and I despaired of ever knowing something so wonderful again. When we lost the battle..." A note of bitterness flavored her words. "When Annalome's weakness failed us all..." Maolan paused, hot tears appearing in her eyes. One fell to the cold stone and hissed as it evaporated.

"When my brother, your dragon, died."

"And Harrana chose human existence to stay with her rider as the veil that protected us formed between the worlds."

"And you chose dragon existence, bringing my brother's body home, but it left you so very alone."

Maolan's eyes closed and tears flowed. "The dragon world has been good to me. I do not regret my life, but I have never lost the loneliness that consumed me at Falong's death along with the loss of our partners, our friends, the dragon-rider pair that completed The

Four."

"And now, you have Harrana again."

Maolan looked sheepishly at her friend. "Masat, in some ways, this has a joy greater than before. I feel revived, connected again to that heart and soul connection of dragon and rider and..."

Masat chuffed in amusement. "And the added bond of lovers."

The emerald green of Maolan's face deepened. Dragons could blush.

"What of Annalome?" Masat asked.

Maolan did not answer immediately. "I know that part of Harrana's heart still longs for her. Sometimes I envy them, the only two to have ever known both the bond of dragon and rider, and the karmic bond of shared lifetimes." She paused, thinking. "I cannot forget that moment of failure, of what Annalome's weakness caused us all. I still hold hate there."

Masat reached out, placing a hand on Maolan's forearm. "But there is still a piece that longs to heal the rift between the three remaining of the Four."

Maolan did not answer. Masat rose to pace slowly in the chamber, finally stopping to stare through the open doorway, apparently absorbed in the blue sky of a cloudless day and the peaks visible on the other side of the river valley that separated the two halves of the high weyr. A transport dragon flew slowly across her line of vision, his massive feet grasping at a net filled with food and other supplies from the rich valley below where wingless earth dragons tended crops and traded with merchants from other realms.

"What if there is more to consider?" Masat asked.

"What do you mean?"

The elder of the two, the dragon mother, turned

to face her friend. A deep intensity showed in her expression and gave added light to her eyes and a deepening of the maroon across her chest.

"It mattered to us all that you were The Four Protectors. Falong is gone. That cannot be changed, but what if it matters to us all that you are now The Three?"

Maolan gasped so deeply that she coughed on the smoke she inhaled from the reservoir of firestone within her. Tears appeared in her eyes once again.

"No one truly knows the depth of the betrayal I feel toward Annalome."

Touching forehead to forehead with the emerald dragon, Masat offered the traditional gesture of comfort before launching the final wave of hurtful words.

"I had suspected," the maroon dragon said. "So, you and Annalome were lovers." It was a statement, not a question.

Maolan's roar released a deep pain, pain from the final exposure of a 10,000-year-old secret.

"Does Harrana know?"

Maolan looked at the stone floor for a long time before answering softly. "She did, but I don't think she remembers. Not yet, at least."

ৡৡৡৡ

The flight had been long toward the north where ice ate at the very earth with a voracious appetite. When the dragon world and human world overlapped, combined, became as one, none had realized the threat of ice to come. Where a plethora of plants and animals had once thrived, now they were pushed either farther south or else they adapted to live in an armed truce with the encroaching cold. Giant woolly mammoths dominated the world as did the hardy plants upon which they subsisted. There were even pockets of humans, dependent on the furs of animals who also survived in the shadow of the ice.

Meekian had sent The Four to observe, to report to him how far the growing ice had progressed or receded. They sought the landmarks he'd designated, cautiously pleased that the ice appeared to have ever so slightly decreased in recent decades. The small council of remaining eastern dragons, the oldest of the old, assured all that the ice would not rule forever, but the two women, the riders of The Four, did not have the perspective of centuries enjoyed by the dragons. Even with their prolonged lives, they would not likely see the end of this age of ice. They valued the adventure of seeing the north, of going beyond where any human now lived, but they would be glad to return to the warm belt around the earth's center where both dragons and humans could thrive.

They had gone as far as Meekian had asked, but it was not a quick and easy journey. The camp each night was cold, unimaginably cold. On this, the third and last night of their frozen mission, a fire blazed on the edge of the half-circle made by the bodies of the sleeping dragons, both curled toward the fire, forming a living shelter for the two women huddled near their bellies. The dragons slept undisturbed by the nearby wall of ice that towered above them. Cold was nothing to a dragon, especially since both had consumed extra firestone before the journey.

"When Meekian said we would be the guardians, I did not think one of our biggest battles would be with the cold," Maolan said.

Annalome laughed. "We have dragons to keep us warm. Who better to send to monitor the ice from the north?"

Despite Maolan's complaints, both women were snuggled warmly in the pocket formed between the two sleeping dragons. Always warm to the touch, their dragon metabolisms had adjusted to the cold, and the humans benefitted by the additional heat exuded by the dragons. Instead of sleeping with each woman wrapped in her own fur-lined cloak, they had made one bed with one cloak beneath and another above, shared body heat adding to their efforts to survive a night so near the massive glacier. During their first night spent actually upon the glacier, both women had suffered miserably with the cold. By the second night, Maolan had suggested the shared bed and shared warmth, but Annalome had only blushed and complained they had not put enough firewood in the nets hung behind their saddles as they flew into fuel less and frozen territory.

Think twice, my rider, Harrana thought, sending only to Annalome's mind.

The unintended response from Annalome was without words, simply the emotions of confusion and shame. Harrana had tugged at Annalome's cloak with one clawed hand, gently encouraging her to agree to Maolan's suggestion.

You are cold, Harrana thought. She knew the source of her rider's fears, for there could be no secrets between dragon and rider. *Your fear is false, dearest.* But Harrana could not force her rider to question the ingrained messages of her village, her father, the elders.

Two sleepless nights were enough. The third night, they shared their cloaks.

"Tonight we have dragon warmth all around,

but my fingers have not forgotten the chill of the long flight," Maolan said.

Annalome rolled toward her companion. She reached for Maolan's hands, raised them to her lips, and blew warmth on cold fingers.

"That helps, but not enough," Maolan said. Brazenly and brusquely, Maolan retrieved her hands and pushed them below the edges of Annalome's tunic to the warmth of the skin beneath.

Annalome gasped. "To the Creator, those fingers are cold," she said.

Maolan rolled to her side, facing the woman beside her. "But they are warming quickly."

She moved the hands from Annalome's warm belly to her sides, then up her back, pulling her companion close as she did so.

"Yes, that is much warmer," Annalome said, breathless.

"Aye, indeed," Maolan answered as she nestled her face in the nape of Annalome's neck. For a moment, the dark-haired woman moved even closer, wrapping her own arms around the warrior, then she stiffened.

"What's wrong?" Maolan asked.

"In my village...I was raised that it is wrong for two women to...to..."

"To love?" Maolan asked. She gazed deeply into Annalome's eyes. "Right or wrong, for me it is too late to question." She took a breath, visibly gathering her courage. "Do not lie to me or to yourself. It is too late for you as well."

They were so close that it required almost no movement for their lips to touch. Maolan was tentative at first, but when Annalome did not pull away, both the kiss and the embrace warmed, the cold outside forgotten for the heat building between them.

"Maolan," Annalome whispered. "If my father knew, the village elders..."

"The village is far away," Maolan answered. "And they are foolish to deny love, whatever its form." She pulled away slightly, reaching to Annalome's face to brush a strand of hair from her eyes. "Can't you see it's not because any God demands it? They simply want your village to grow, to have children, to sanction the love only between a man and woman to ensure those children. We are riders, sweet Annalome. To bear children is to take us from the duty we have to protect all."

"They must never know," Annalome said. "My family, the village..."

"They must never know," Maolan mumbled as she nuzzled at the neck of her companion and lover.

Annalome pulled her even closer. She buried her face in Maolan's hair.

"And I have wanted this for a long time," she said.

"And I as well," Maolan responded.

The kiss was long and led to so much more. When the pleasure they gave each other became intense, the connectivity of heart and mind between dragon and rider reached to the sleeping dragons beside them, and the cold, dark night was filled with the sounds of dragon purrs as they celebrated the pleasure of their riders.

Maolan had not allowed herself that memory for centuries. She wept.

Masat held Maolan closely, comforting her as she had so often her child.

"What if..." Maolan started.

"Yes?"

Maolan sat up abruptly, looking intently at the older dragon. "What if it was shame at our love that weakened Annalome's hand in the battle?"

A sigh preceded Masat's response. "Now I understand the hate you've held, you've nurtured. The hate shielded you from feeling the love."

More tears were Maolan's only answer.

Chapter Four

Original Mission

Kidwell stared at the computer monitor for a long time, tears teasing at her eyes. The morning news from Reuters, her preferred source, displayed before her. She recalled so clearly the fall of the Berlin Wall. Like so many, at that moment she knew a relief from a fear and dread she had carried from her earliest childhood. Every child of her age could recognize a mushroom cloud, regularly heard the news too heavy for young minds about the devastation that nuclear war would mean.

"Have they learned nothing?" Kidwell asked the empty room.

A petty scratching match continued between the current president and the dictator at a country established as a longtime enemy of the US. Each man now threatened the other with nuclear reprisals. Kidwell wondered if either of these little boys in men's bodies had any clue what their childish argument could mean for all of humanity, for the very earth itself.

Why don't they just drop their pants and compare dick sizes?

Perhaps she shouldn't have read the day's news. It had been a tough night. Kidwell knew the process, even welcomed it, despite the physical and emotional drain. Some called it a Dark Night of the Soul. Prior experience comforted Kidwell, but that did not eliminate the pain, the confusion, the discomfort. Every night for nearly two weeks some internal force drug her out of the warm blanket of sleep and into a swirl of unexplained emotions and flashes of images. Some she recognized as past traumas in this life or prior lives. Many had absolutely nothing to do with her life or experiences, but she felt a certainty that they belonged to someone. Always these episodes came between three and four a.m.—the witching hour.

The first time Kidwell plunged into a Dark Night of the Soul she struggled, striving to identify the cause of each emotion, the message behind each image. She believed a scientific, psychological model provided the answer. Some things healed: the long-forgotten terror as a small child when she'd been left, forgotten in a strange store, after each parent thought she was in the company of the other; the ear-popping physicality of a too-near explosion when she served in the Middle East followed by the cotton-mouthed horror while striving to help bloody comrades unfortunate enough to be not near but in those explosions—some maimed, some dead. Kidwell now knew and understood the ecstasy and the pain when a fractured piece of her soul came home to reunite with the entirety that was Kidwell. Coming home were those pieces that departed to hold trauma too awful to be faced in the moment of reality. With each retrieval, life became easier. Small events no longer became huge triggers, so that the pop of a firecracker no longer forced Kidwell's heart into racing mode.

In time, Kidwell learned that the Dark Night of the Soul covered bigger territory than individual traumas. She gained the skill of simply relaxing into the experience. This soul process was beyond the understanding of the mind. She suspected a tie to connectivity of all creation, of accepting her tiny place in that matrix and allowing the healing of her piece. As she accepted that, the episodes shortened and she could attain, at least momentarily, that transcendence when everything mattered and nothing mattered.

Kidwell leaned back, her decrepit office chair creaking with the motion. She rested her head against the back of the chair, eyes closed, and a tear trickled from her right eye downward and into her ear.

"Okay, that's enough," Kidwell said aloud.

She sat up abruptly, efficiently going through the steps of shutting down the computer. Before the screen was totally blank, she stood, walking toward the back door off the kitchen. She kicked off her house shoes and pulled her hiking boots from the rack near the door, sitting in a kitchen chair to slip on and lace the boots. There was an air of determination as she left the house, closing the door solidly behind her. She knew where to go, and her steps took her to a worn path to a nearby place that had become holy for them not long after Kidwell and Anna moved to their mountain home. For Kidwell, it still was.

The darkness from her nighttime challenges eased as she walked, noting a red-tailed hawk drifting above, finally easing down to its nest in a nearby oak in the meadow beside the creek and outside the line of pine trees that covered the mountainside. She breathed deeply of the pine scent as the path led into the shadow of the trees, and she made directly for the "fairy throne." She and Anna had christened it such many years ago, noting the natural seat created by a curved root from the pine tree that provided the back to the throne. The earth within the curve of the root formed a comfortable seat, especially after the years of Kidwell and company taking a seat at the throne seeking peace and meditation. In time, the earth had formed a natural basin ideal for human anatomy. The ground dropped away from the root, providing a perfect level for a person to rest their feet as they sat upon the "throne." The creek was nearby, and the bubble of moving water mixed with the hushed whisper of wind in the pines.

Kidwell sat. That is all, she just sat. The smell of the woods, the sound of the water, the caw of nearby crows, all of it washed over her, easing the ache of heart and soul, restoring some of the peace lost during the night's battles and the reading of the morning news. She closed her eyes, focusing on the cool air on her skin, the perfume of her mountain, and the soft sounds of nature.

I should do this more often.

"Yes, you should," a man's voice answered.

Kidwell turned, surprised, to see him seated no more than two feet to her left. He sat comfortably on the earth, his legs pulled up under his rough-spun robe, and his bearded face resting on his knees. His arms were wrapped around his legs, and he smiled gently at Kidwell.

Kidwell looked around, surprised and confused. This was not her first vision of Jesus, but before it had always been an astral experience. She had even viewed her own body abandoned temporarily below.

"What do you seek?" he asked.

"It feels like I'm still in my body," she said.

"You are."

She reached out hesitantly, touching his arm. "You're flesh."

"Yes, I am," he responded, a hint of irony in his voice.

"How is that possible?"

He raised his head from his knees, shaking it gently and smiling teasingly. "Possible? You of all people wonder what's possible?"

Kidwell laughed, embarrassed. "Yeah, I guess it's a surprise when miracles take a new form, even for someone accustomed to miracles."

"Do you need proof of who I am?" he asked, extending his left hand toward her. She could see the open wound on his wrist.

"I'm not Thomas," she said. "I know who you are." Kidwell turned her attention to the sky, and she tilted her head to one side, listening.

"What do you seek?" he asked again.

"I'm looking for the beams of light, people ascending into heaven. I'm listening for trumpets."

"The Second Coming?"

"Why, yes."

Jesus laughed so hard tears came to his eyes. "It's amazing the images people create to make prophecies appear as they wish." He wiped a tear from his eye with the sleeve of his robe. "Dear Kidwell, I never really left."

His laughter was contagious. Kidwell found herself chuckling without really knowing why.

"We are a silly lot, aren't we?" she asked.

"Humanity?"

"Yes."

"Oh, Kidwell, it is true that you all have brought me much joy and laughter." His face turned serious.

"And even more anxiety and pain."

"Like now?"

"Yes, but you also bring me hope," he said.

Kidwell grasped a twig from the ground and nervously broke it into tiny pieces. "Why me?"

"Why the burden of prophecy, of being a guardian?"

"Yes." She turned to him. "I'll do my best, but you know I'm not up to the job." She thought of the petty argument threatening nuclear destruction. "I can't solve humanity's problems."

"Nor could I."

Kidwell looked at him, astonished. "What? But you died for our sins. That gave humanity hope."

He looked at her with a hint of skepticism. "Did I die for your sins, or because of your sins?"

"What do you mean?"

"Why do people assume that my life and death were predestined? Why do people assume the cross was the only possible outcome?"

She couldn't breathe. Kidwell stared at the deity become man, her whole world suddenly knocked off its axis. A profound grief consumed her. It felt that she bore a burden of guilt for all of humanity.

"Oh, dear God!"

"Yes?"

A hilarity verging on hysteria hit Kidwell as she realized exactly what she had just said and to whom. She laughed and cried at the same time. For the first time in her life, Kidwell realized that she had not the ability to stop either the laughter or the tears. At that moment, she feared herself in a way she did not realize was possible.

Jesus looked at her, concerned. He gently placed

a hand on the top of her head.

"Peace," he whispered in command. The hysteria left Kidwell, and she felt a deep and profound quiet.

"I am so, so sorry," she said. "You gave us your all, and we betrayed you."

"You betrayed yourselves," he responded. "Humanity is capable of so much, both good and evil. It is the freedom of choice that is the tool for achieving your full potential."

"But we are an amalgamation of individuals. How can the species ever achieve full potential when we can't even agree on what to call...well, you?"

He laughed. "When enough of you chose love, learn to listen to the spirit within you instead of the manipulators outside you. Perhaps, perhaps the time is close."

"What should I do?" she asked.

"Your best," he answered. "You can only be responsible for yourself, but, maybe by example you can help others believe in doing their best."

"Critical mass?"

"Yes, to use a scientific term."

Kidwell blushed. "I hope that's not offensive to you."

He laughed again. Kidwell was realizing how fond he was of laughter.

"Science does not offend me. Humanity strives to understand the universe. How could that be offensive?" His face became stern. "It is offensive when some strive to silence questioning minds and hearts in my name."

"I suspected as much." She paused, listening to a fresh call of nearby crows flying overhead. "Why are you here, today?"

He touched her hand gently. "Because we have

placed a great burden on you. I saw your pain, and I wanted you to know you do not bear this burden alone."

Quiet tears filled her eyes. "Thank you."

"There is more."

"Yes?"

"It is good that you seek to cage the lions that prey on others. Still, it is wiser to befriend the lions, to decrease the number of renegades who can corrupt the entire pride."

Kidwell looked at him with a half smile. "You still speak in parables?"

"Always," he responded. "What good is an answer given if a person does not go through the process of finding it for herself?"

He stood, and Kidwell followed. They faced each other, and he placed a hand on the side of her face.

"Be good to yourself, Kidwell Brown—Harrana the dragon. Never forget that you are not alone in your struggles."

Kidwell closed her eyes as he leaned forward to kiss her on the top of the head. When she opened them again, he was gone. She began the walk back to her home. As she walked, she realized it was time to renew her writing for *The Book of Kidwell*.

Chapter Five

The Tables Turn, Again

Only here, in a cavern so deep that humanity had no hope of ever reaching the dark magic, could the Governor walk on two huge legs and feel the cold stone and gritty earth beneath the leathery souls of his clawed feet. It had taken millennia for those demons caught in this universe to find this tiny pocket exempt from the magic that doomed them to a half existence, ethereal and unable to physically influence the world around them. Only through their influence on the minds and souls of corporeal beings, especially the mixed-bag souls of humanity, were they able to work their magic. The Governor's only hope of ever returning to his home world required that he win a battle begun 10,000 years before.

The Governor lived in those caverns along with his wife, a human woman corrupted so long ago that there was no longer a discernable difference between herself and the demons she had joined. They had lived in the caverns for over two centuries, accompanied by only a handful of servants and guards. Here they enjoyed a nearly permanent existence as physical beings. Others dreaded being called to the caverns, for it was rare to stand before the Governor without facing some form of displeasure or punishment. The worst involved those rare occasions when a portal would open to their home universe, now a one-way trip reserved for those to face eternal punishment for their failures.

Once outside the huge and barren meeting cavern, the Governor entered their living cave, amazingly beautiful compared to its occupants. His once beautiful wife never entirely lost her human soul, including the lust for wealth and beauty that had been much of her downfall. A mix of fine furnishings, rugs, and art filled the cave, pieces stolen from throughout human history. Persian and Navajo rugs adorned floors and walls, and sculptures and magnificent pottery were scattered throughout, many of which would solve long-held mysteries of missing fine art.

The Governor grasped a vase from its pedestal and launched it across the room, roaring in anger as he did so. Despite her size and bulk, his wife moved with phenomenal speed and grace, delicately catching the vase before it hit the wall. She emitted a noise that was somewhere between a growl and a purr. She studied the enameled pottery, looking closely for any sign of damage.

"Ming dynasty, you know," she said to her husband, her lip curled in distaste.

"I preferred the Mongols," he responded.

"You would. They were far better at creating destruction than art." She placed the vase back on its pedestal and then gently moved them both to a more protected location. "What troubles you, husband?"

"Another of my greatest conquests has been captured."

The wife continued the conversation a safe distance from her angry husband. "How?"

"I've sent Belzabulb to investigate. We have

no clue. Twice now my very best human servants have been magically taken from their safeholds and imprisoned, awaiting trial in that damn World Court."

"Magic?" she asked. "I thought that was nearly dead among the humans."

"As did I," he answered. "But I know no other answer." The sound of a huge gong interrupted. "That must be him now. Go. Bring him here."

"Here? I hate your minions in our space. They hate things of beauty."

"Go!" he yelled. The Governor dropped to a seat on a massive stone chair. He knew better than to sit on any of the fine furniture around him. Although it pleased his eye in a way he would confess only to his wife, he knew that each piece was useless beneath his great weight.

Mumbling unhappily, the wife left the chamber, scurrying to obey her husband. When she returned, she was followed by a tall and gangly demon.

"What did you find?" the Governor demanded.

"Still no clue how it was done," Belzabulb said. "It was the same, though, taken from his bed as he slept with no sign of how they passed guards, locked doors, and windows."

The Governor leaned forward, so angry his eyes glowed red. "So, you found nothing?"

As Belzabulb smiled, a drop of drool escaped his lips leaving a huge damp stain on the fine rug beneath. "I did find something," he said.

"What?"

The gawky demon rubbed his hands together and shifted from foot to foot. "I smelled something I haven't smelled for millennia."

"What? Say it," the Governor demanded.

"Dragon," his lieutenant said. "I smelled a hint of dragon."

The Governor's eyes turned blue, a cold blue. It was the color of fear.

Belzabulb began to undulate his upper body, reminiscent of a frightened snake in an offensive stance. "There's more."

"What?" He had chosen this lieutenant as spy because of his keen smell and acute memory.

"I remember the specific scent." He leaned close to the Governor, hissing in a whisper. "It was one of the Four."

The Governor's eyes became even bluer, like a pale sky. "One of the Four who came so near to closing the portal, the two great dragons and their riders?"

"Yessssssss."

"They're dead," the Governor shouted.

"Noooooo."

"Then we'll have to do something about that." The Governor was deeply troubled. He had worked so long to attain the near perfect positioning of human converts in key positions. He could almost smell the victory of final conquest, but a cold fear filled his already cold heart. If any of the Four lived, the outcome was not so certain.

✦ ✦ ✦ ✦

A wooden brooch looked incongruous where it was pinned on Kidwell's plain black T-shirt. It was a miniature of the dragon's eye that hung in her bedroom. Aisha had expressed concern when Maolan asked her to create it.

"My magic paintings, they always come from

inspiration, not intent," Aisha had said.

"Please, friend of my love," Maolan responded. "If she must walk alone into danger, we need a way to see where she is, what is happening."

Aisha's forehead creased with worry. "I agree," she answered. "Let me meditate and pray, seek the inspiration. I shall ask for the magic."

It worked. Even Aisha had been surprised at the results. She walked into her studio, expecting to sit in quiet meditation and prayer for as long as it took. Instead, she walked directly to a box of wood bits and stones she had collected during her many stays at Kidwell's mountain home. On the top of the stack was a wood scrap, eye-shaped, and immediate inspiration moved her hands with brush and paint to create an almost identical miniature of the dragon's eye painting. What's more, it was a portal. Masat and Maolan could watch from the portal window in Allana's bed cavern. When Kidwell wore the brooch, they could see the sights around her as though they possessed an eye upon her shoulder. In a sense, they did. All were shocked when they carried the test a step further, with Kidwell taking dragon form while wearing the brooch. It transformed with her, and her dragon family and companion could see and hear all that she saw and heard as her dragon self.

"Thank you," Maolan said to Aisha after telling her the extent of the brooch's magic. Aisha's face reflected shock and pleasure as the Celtic warrior and dragon rider tenderly embraced the artist, a vulnerability she rarely showed anyone. "Now she need not walk totally alone."

Aisha pushed the other woman gently to arm's length so that she could see the warrior's face. "Thank you for protecting my sister in ways I cannot," she said.

Today would be the real test. Kidwell fingered the brooch nervously until Maolan slapped her hand away.

"Don't do that," Maolan drawled. "If your hand is over the eye, we canna see."

Kidwell laughed without humor. "True. Guess that's a nervous habit I need to avoid."

Maolan glowered at her lover. "Aye, it is."

Instead, Kidwell put her hand in her pocket, nervously fiddling with the slick case protecting the memory stick hidden there. If they succeeded in the day's plans, that tiny piece of technology could ensure the life and well-being of many.

Kidwell felt no animosity at Maolan's stern anger. She knew the love and concern behind it. Taking a deep breath, Kidwell calmed herself, striving to conceal the unease she felt as she prepared for her next mission, her newest assignment from Roberto of the World Court. The weapons dealer she had captured was a pragmatic man. When he realized the full extent of his plight, he offered the only bargaining tool likely to improve his situation: information. He told what he could from memory, details about his customers, their plans and resources, all in exchange for a cushy sentence in a minimum-security facility. He remembered much, but details were lacking. For that he gave the location of his personal laptop, along with passwords and file names. All helpful stuff with one major obstacle—the placing of an agent within the closely guarded confines of the luxurious haven provided to the arms dealer by his primary benefactor. For that they needed Kidwell and her truly unique skills and talents.

This would be no quick in and out. She would need to not only take human form but also take time, precious time, to locate the computer, download the designated files, and replace the computer so that no clue remained of her visit. On prior missions, Kidwell had not known the metallic taste of fear, but she knew it now, something she strove to hide from Maolan and Martin as they waited for the designated time of her teleportation.

Kidwell had moved the dragon eye from her bedroom to living room. She temporarily removed a painting she and Anna had purchased at the Spanish Market in Santa Fe many years earlier, hanging the eye in its prominent place. Maolan planned to return to the dragon lair where Masat and Allana lived so that she could monitor Kidwell's mission, but the only channel Martin had for any news of the outcome would be through the eye as Maolan and Masat shared what they saw. Far away in Texas, Aisha and Greg sat anxiously by the telephone, waiting for Martin to call.

"It's nearly time," Kidwell said, looking at her watch for the hundredth time. The arms dealer had given them the best window of opportunity, when the guards would be lax as the rest of the compound slept.

"I will go now and watch from the weyr," Maolan said. Before willing herself to flow through the eye, Maolan held Kidwell tenderly. They kissed.

While Kidwell focused on the parting with her friend and lover, she was not totally unaware of Martin's discomfort. Her heart hurt knowing that the young man may never free himself of seeing Kidwell and Anna as a single unit, the mothers of his heart. She knew also that she would never be fully free of that bond even as she felt joy and gratitude for the love she shared with Maolan.

Maolan's form changed, and she flowed like mercury through the eye. Kidwell and Martin now looked through the window, seeing three dragons waiting on the other side.

"Take care, my sister," the dragon mother said while her daughter, Kidwell's adopted niece, only hummed and danced with barely contained anxiety.

"Let's light this candle," Kidwell said. She gave Martin's arm a squeeze and directed what she hoped was a reassuring smile his direction. She picked up the drawing Roberto had provided, a detailed image of the room where she was to teleport. Barely a moment's concentration was required before her form flashed to a different shape, a downsized version of her dragon self, long enough for Martin to barely see the black form with rainbow highlights, like the feathers of a raven. Then she was gone.

🐉🐉🐉🐉🐉

"Wake! Wake, you useless minion," a voice shouted.

The chief of guards sat up in his bed, sweating from the nightmare. The vision of a grotesque face from his dream hung in his mind, inflicting a fear the war-hardened captain-of-the-guard rarely felt. Perhaps his fear receptors were still highly sensitive, aware at how close his master had come to ordering his execution when their "guest" had simply disappeared in the night. The man swung his legs off the edge of the bed. Shaking his head to clear his sleep-fuzzy thoughts, he wondered what to do. After all, it was just a dream.

❧ ❧ ❧ ❧

As her dragon-self, Kidwell had only a flash of visibility when she appeared in the strange suite of expensively furnished rooms. She stayed dragon, using her species' ability to manipulate electromagnetism to create an illusion of invisibility. She looked around the rooms, finding no one. She was surprised to see that the weapons dealer had apparently not lied about the absence of security cameras in his suite. As invisible dragon, she walked to the painting she had been assured covered a wall safe. With dragon hands she removed the painting, finding the safe and awkwardly working the combination. She saw stacks of documents and cash within, objects about which she cared nothing. Atop them all was the object of her search, a compact and expensive laptop computer.

Now the real risk began. To manipulate the computer, she must be human. To be human, she must be visible. Kidwell willed the change, and she stood before the open safe visible to anyone who knew to look. She prayed no one would look. Working as quickly as possible, she removed the computer and moved toward a nearby desk. She breathed a sigh of relief as she opened the laptop, hit the power button, and it started. One of her greatest fears had been that it would be without charge, requiring time to connect it to power. As it rested on the desk, Kidwell entered the password she had memorized, and there it was, desktop open and each file available for her retrieval. She plugged the memory stick into a USB port, opened the file manager, and systematically copied the key file folders to the flash drive. All went smoothly and as planned. Kidwell had already lapsed into the mindset she had known before in combat and as a firefighter. The fear was gone. All emotion was gone, for that matter. A cold part of her mind controlled every thought and motion; where the outside moved with amazing speed, her thoughts felt slow and methodical.

No expense had been spared on the computer, and the transfer happened rapidly. Within only a few minutes, Kidwell had the memory stick back in her pocket and shut down the computer. It was back in the safe, and she was lifting the painting from where it leaned against the wall. Within moments she would be standing safely in Roberto's office handing him the precious computer files.

The front door burst open with a bang, followed immediately by another bang, one that tore through Kidwell's left shoulder like a miniature hurricane and wildfire all in one. She hit the wall with the force of the bullet, rotating as she did so, sliding down and struggling to pull the Walther .380—the one Martin had insisted she carry—from the holster on her belt. She pulled it so fast that the round she fired went wild, hitting the wall three feet to the left of the burly guard still standing in the doorway, but it made him duck, causing his second shot to go wild as well. She could hear voices shouting from the hallway.

That's when another explosive force slammed Kidwell against the wall once again, but this time it came from the brooch on her shirt. She saw a mercury flow of emerald green, then the scales of a dragon so close she could only see a fragment of the beast in front of her.

Maolan, she thought with a combination of

relief for herself and fear for Maolan. Then a wall of fire—dragon fire—filled the room. Kidwell heard the agonized screams of the man in the doorway. Then she felt mind connect with mind, and Maolan was with her. She saw the sudden image of a cave mouth overlooking a green valley far below.

Take us there, she heard Maolan's voice in her mind.

Through the pain and confusion Kidwell grasped that image, and fear and instinct guided her as she touched the dragon before her creating a physical and metaphysical bond, flowing immediately into dragon form and teleportation. She barely had time to feel the cold stone of the cave floor as her form returned to human, an injured and broken human. Her universe faded to black as she lost consciousness.

Chapter Six

Enlightenment

No!" Anna screamed. She sat up in her narrow bed, sobbing as she did so. "No, Kidwell, no!"

Anna's hand went automatically to her left shoulder, feeling a residual burn in both front and back, sympathy pains for the entrance and exit wounds she had just experienced in her dream where she simultaneously watched and was the woman who was her soulmate, the soulmate she had betrayed so profoundly.

"She lives," a melodic voice said in the darkness.

Turning to her right, she saw the faint glow of an angel where he sat, unperturbed, in a straight-backed chair by her bed. It was not the first time Anna had seen this angel, so she felt limited surprise.

"How bad is she hurt?" she asked.

"All in due time," the angel answered. "You two still have a task before you."

"I'm not strong enough," Anna wailed. "I've never been strong enough."

"No one is alone," he answered. "You are not alone." Both the sound and vision faded to nothing as he spoke his last words.

Anna sat breathing deeply, striving to slow her thumping heart. There was a light knock on the door.

Anna swung her bare feet onto the wooden floor of the roughly finished barn room she had claimed for herself. Her gratitude to the Martinez family for taking her in did not prevent her from asking to leave the house, to take this simple room filled with the smell of fresh hay stacked just the other side of the wall. She needed solitude as she sought comfort and healing. Anna shrugged on a light bathrobe and turned on the small lamp on the nightstand before crossing the room to the door.

"*¿Estas bien, Hita?*" asked the old woman standing outside, the porch light from the main house shining behind. "I heard you calling all the way in the house." She, too, wore a robe, one Anna recognized as the man's robe once worn by Señora Martinez's late husband.

"*No, Abuela. No estoy bien,*" Anna answered. "I have had a dream, a horrible dream."

The old woman reached to gently embrace Anna. "Come inside, child. We will make warm milk and you can tell me about the dream."

"But you need your sleep, Abuela," Anna answered.

The old woman chuckled. "The sleep of the old is frequently a broken thing. The milk will help me as well."

Across the yard, a light turned on and a well-muscled man stepped onto the porch of a double-wide trailer, pulling up the braces from the suspenders on his jeans as he did so. His home was part of the hodgepodge structures of the family compound. The abuela's home, an ancient adobe structure, was the flagship, with the center core built more than two centuries earlier by the first of the family to settle the land.

"Are you all right, Mama?" he called.

"*Bien,* Alfredo," she answered.

"You okay, Anna?" he asked.

"Just a dream," Anna answered. "I'm sorry I woke you."

The man waved absently, then shuffled sleepily back into his house.

The two women walked together across the yard toward the main house. Once inside, they worked with concerted familiarity around the small kitchen, Anna retrieving the glass jug of milk—fresh from the cow Anna had milked that morning—from the refrigerator while the old woman retrieved an old and battered pan from where it hung with others on the wall. Anna gathered powdered cocoa, sugar, and a small container of finely ground red chili while the abuela measured two cups of milk into the pan that she placed on a burner on the gas stove. The wood stove that so long served the Martinez family still filled much of one wall of the kitchen. Anna smiled as she looked at it, remembering fondly the wonderful odor when Abuela Martinez had fired up the old stove last fall to make traditional *chicos* from the fresh garden corn. With a spoon, the abuela placed cocoa, sugar, and a small amount of chili into the heating milk.

"I'll do that, Abuela," Anna said as she gently took the wooden spoon from the older woman. "Sit at the table. I'll bring the milk." Wearily, the old woman obeyed.

"Tell me about your dream," Señora Martinez commanded.

Anna closed her eyes and took a deep breath. "I don't think it was just a dream."

"Probably not. Tell me."

Anna's hand shook as she stirred the milk. "In the dream"—she took a deep breath—"Kidwell was shot."

"*Madre de Dios*," the old woman responded, crossing herself. "Was she...? Is she...?"

Anna hesitated. Even with this old woman who was now the mother of her heart, she felt odd sharing something many would think insane. "I awoke to an angel sitting beside me. He told me she lives."

"Is that all?"

"I asked how bad she was hurt. He just said, 'In due time.'"

"Then, in the morning, you must call the *indio*. I don't remember his name."

"Martin. You're right, I must." Anna chewed gently at her lower lip. She dreaded the call. She still felt so much shame at what she'd done, and she could hear the disappointment in Martin's voice whenever they spoke. "Or maybe calling Aisha would be wiser."

Anna poured the milk from the pan into two waiting cups, placed the pan in the sink and filled it with water, then carried both cups to the table. They sat sipping in companionable silence. It was not the first time these two women had sat at this table discussing things they could share with no other.

"You will always love her?" the abuela asked.

"Of course," Anna answered. "We have shared many lives together."

"I am sorry for what my daughter did," the old woman said. She knew her daughter, Celia, had systematically seduced Anna, preying on her fear and insecurity while Kidwell was away.

"We did it together," Anna responded. Tears

teased at her eyes as she remembered. Kidwell had been away for many months, on a mission to help people in the Yucatan being used by a cruel and powerful drug lord. Celia Martinez had come to work as the groundskeeper. Martin had warned her of the woman's intentions, but Anna had not listened. Celia had a way of looking into Anna's heart, of seeing and building the fire of Anna's secret doubts, of her fear that she did not have the strength and courage to be the wife of a Prophet. Anna was still mystified at who she became for those moments, her life's ultimate weakness, when Celia had enticed Anna into her bed. She remembered the night when Kidwell found them there and her whole life turned upside down.

As though she could read her mind, the old woman placed a gnarled hand over Anna's. "You are not the person you were then."

"No," Anna agreed. "I'm not."

Sometimes Anna wondered if all that drama and pain had been to bring her here, to find the abuela and the healing and strength she discovered in the very family who spawned the woman who had been her downfall, for the failure of this life had led to her memory of the original failure. She had begun to wonder if the time had finally come to heal an ancient karma.

"Tell me the story again," the old woman said.

"The story?" Anna smiled, pretending she did not understand.

"Of the battle, of your time as a dragon rider."

Anna was still amazed at how easily the abuela accepted the revived memory of her original life. And so, Anna told the tale again. She relived the days of being rider to the mystical dragon Harrana, of the bond between them and the other dragon-rider pair, Maolan and Falong, who were their constant companions. With pain, she told of her failure in the great battle, when she bore the burden of closing the portal after the demons had found an opening into this world. She told of the closing of the veils between the worlds and the lesser magic that robbed the demons of physical form and closed the doors between the human world and others to protect the spread of the demons. There was a hint of daylight through the window as she finished, and she realized that the abuela was half asleep in her chair.

Chapter Seven

Alive!

Kidwell regretted drifting back to conscious-ness. It hurt. Blissful darkness had been a better option. She tried to sit up, an action which triggered new pain and made her see a whole sky full of stars behind her eyelids.

"Ouch," she mumbled. She would have rather screamed, but that would hurt too much.

Her right hand drifted up to her left shoulder and encountered a thick covering there—to stem the blood, she was sure. She shifted slightly and realized another pad covered the exit wound on her back. She sniffed at the covering. *Moss,* she thought, recognizing Maolan's healing touch and knowledge. She was covered in a wool cloak she also recognized as Maolan's. She held it to her face, breathing in the comforting scent of the Irishwoman. Her hand drifted from the shoulder toward her neck, feeling along the bone ridge.

Broken collar bone. Damn. No wonder I can't sit up. She recalled when she'd been a young lieutenant junior grade stationed at Naval Station Ingelside in Texas. A shipmate persuaded her to discover the joys of enduro motorcycles. Almost every weekend she and her friend hit the trails. She especially enjoyed doing doughnuts on a patch of sandy land, a pleasure that ended the day she flew over the handlebars, zipped beyond the sand, and landed on hard ground. Luckily, they were near a road. She didn't have to walk far to meet up with the ambulance. The worst moment had been rising from the ground, made possible only with the help of her friend. Lesson learned then and remembered now. She wouldn't be sitting up without help, and, once up, she didn't plan to lie down again anytime soon.

Kidwell looked around, trying to orient herself. She had a vague memory of the image Maolan had planted in her mind giving her a teleportation destination. Near to her right was the rough wall of a cave, but it was too dark for her to see the wall to her left or the ceiling above. A torch, appearing hastily made from a stick and the same moss that covered her wounds, sputtered nearby, putting out little light. As she looked around, the cave began to lighten, and Kidwell could see she was only a few yards from the entrance. A new day dawned outside.

Glad I lived to see it, and a little surprised I did. Without thinking, she made a vague effort to sit up again, desiring to better see her surroundings, and she moaned with the pain. *Remember, no sitting without help.* She tried to see more, her mind focusing on one primary thought. *Where's Maolan?* As though in answer, she heard the familiar sound of dragon wings, and she saw a shadow flash across the entrance. Kidwell felt a relief so intense it brought tears to her eyes, in its way affecting her far more than the pain.

Now in human form, Maolan rushed into the cave. Light nearly filled the enclosure, and Kidwell saw that she now carried an electric camp lantern. In her other hand was a stainless-steel water bottle. She was dressed for battle as she had so very long ago.

Leather and chainmail covered her. Maolan laid down her burdens and threw iron helmet, sword, and shield to the side. She dropped to her knees, and Kidwell could see her lover's face was pale, her cheeks a bright red. Maolan reached to brush sweat-dampened hair from Kidwell's face.

"*Eudail*, you're awake," Maolan said, breathless with fear.

"Thank you," Kidwell said, barely audible, her voice raspy and dry.

"Here, drink this," Maolan said, fumbling with the unfamiliar water bottle.

"Flip the top up. I hope it has a straw." It did. Maolan held it to her and Kidwell drank greedily until Maolan pulled it away.

"Not too much. We dunna want ya to get sick," Maolan said.

Kidwell cringed at the very thought of the pain retching would cause. "No, we don't." She grasped Maolan's hand with her own and held it to her cheek. "Thank you for saving me."

"I should have gone with ya," Maolan said, a hint of reproach in her voice. Kidwell wasn't sure toward whom the reproach was directed.

"I heard wings...I didn't know you could be dragon here."

"I didn't, either," Maolan responded. "When I saw—" She paused as though fighting for breath. "When I saw you shot, I just acted. Never planned nor intended what I did."

Kidwell gasped and felt frantically toward her left shoulder.

"Don't you dare disturb that poultice. Had a time getting the bleeding to stop. I found some yarrow, too, and packed it in to help with the pain."

"The eye? The brooch?" Kidwell asked.

"Destroyed. All our lot in both worlds must be desperate wondering what happened. Thanks be it held together long enough for me to make it through. I fear the power of my coming shattered it more than the bullet."

"Perhaps I could teleport—"

"Dunna even think it," Maolan commanded in a voice not to be questioned. "You'll do nothing but be nurtured for some time to come."

Kidwell looked around the cave again. "Where are we?"

"It's changed a mite over the millennia, but dunna you recognize it?"

Kidwell looked again and felt a vague familiarity. She closed her eyes and welcomed the vision of memory. "It's Falong's weyr, the one he used when you'd go back to visit your village. Sometimes we'd come too."

"It's all I could think of in the haste, needing a haven. I should have thought of your home, but I was acting, not thinking," Maolan said.

"Is there still a village?"

"Aye, although more like a city if it were back in those times. A town now, I guess. That's where I was when I left." She caressed Kidwell's cheek. "Help is on the way, but they had to wait for daylight to start the hike. Help is coming."

"They know the way?"

Maolan laughed. "Know the way? It's a favorite hike. Guess what they call this place?"

"What?"

"The Dragon Cave. Aye, I'm not lying."

Kidwell's laugh was cut short by a wave of pain. "They didn't see you?"

"Nay, *Eudail*. Dragons remain a legend here. I flew down in the dark and turned human before I saw a car with the lights on top. Like the ones I've seen through a portal when I could view one of the magic boxes."

"Television."

"Anyway, I woke the poor blighter who was catching a nap inside. Told him I had a friend injured in the cave above the village. He used that talking box in the car and pretty soon a passel of vehicles with flashing lights showed up, one was a white box, the ones that take sick people to see the shaman."

"An ambulance."

"Yes, one of those. Anyway, the blighter who'd been copping a nap had lots of questions, and I answered as best I could. He was especially keen when I told him you were shot, and he was downright rude about what I was wearing and the sword and shield on my back."

"Lucky they didn't arrest you."

"Ah, dear heart, I learned something important. I pulled him close and told him it was Kidwell Brown lying injured in their Dragon Cave. His eyes went wide as saucers, and he said as how his wife read to him from your book before they went to sleep at night. Your name has its own magic now."

"A mixed blessing."

"Anyway, I heard them planning, and when I knew they wouldn't be leaving before daylight, I slipped away into the dark and flew back to you."

Kidwell shivered involuntarily. *Shock*, Kidwell thought, saying nothing.

"My poor darlin'," Maolan said. She pulled the chainmail and tunic over her head, and wriggled out of her breeches and boots, now dressed only in a light cotton shift. She lifted the cloak and lay beside Kidwell, covering them both under the warm material. She carefully wrapped arms and legs around Kidwell, striving not to cause her pain. Almost immediately, Kidwell felt the physical as well as the emotional warmth of her lover. The shivering slowed, gradually abating. She found herself drifting to sleep, and as she did so there was a strange vision, somewhere between memory and dream. There was surprise somewhere, but she had not strength nor will to feel it completely. With certainty, she knew this was not the first time two women had shared the warmth of this cloak, and in the dream she caught a vague whiff of the distinct scent of Anna in the woolen cloth.

☙ ☙ ❧ ❧

The paramedic knew what he was doing. Kidwell was pleasantly surprised at how little pain he caused as he lifted her to a sitting position so that he could examine both entrance and exit wounds. His brow creased as he gently removed the moss and yarrow poultices from front and back. He examined both, carefully removing the moss bandages with hands covered in protective medical gloves. Glancing back and forth between the wounds, he allowed himself a slight smile as he examined the moss pads.

"Not exactly standard procedure, but it certainly did the job," he said.

He cleaned and bandaged both wounds, and then used copious amounts of self-adhering bandage followed with strategically placed strips of surgical tape to immobilize the collar bone. Kidwell felt immediate relief which became total relief as he administered an emergency ampule of morphine.

"It will make the trip down better for us all," he explained.

As he worked, the man communicated via radio with a doctor in the hospital in the village. Between her pain, exhaustion, and the morphine, Kidwell couldn't understand a word of their heavy brogues, especially as the occasional smattering of Gaelic peppered the conversation. A cadre of firefighters shuffled near the entrance, standing near the Stokes Basket they'd carried up the mountain with them. Kidwell counted the men and women of the group—twelve. She knew from her own firefighting days that there were far more than needed to carry the basket at one time, but they would need everyone before the trip was completed. Carrying a person on a mountain trail was exhausting and sometimes dangerous. As the paramedic worked, she almost suggested rope or tubular webbing as harness for the carriers at front and back. Before she could speak, one firefighter pulled a length of webbing and began expertly fashioning just such a harness.

I'm in good hands.

After Kidwell was duly packaged and medicated, the paramedic gently pinched the skin on her hand. He watched closely for the time it took for the skin to return to its normal position.

"Hydration looks good." He turned to Maolan. "You did a fine job of stopping the bleeding. I'll check her now and again, but I don't think we'll need an IV for the trip down." He turned to the firefighters. "Up to you lads and lasses now. Let's get her down."

"I hear it's Kidwell Brown herself we'll be carrying," one young woman said.

"Aye," Maolan answered. "And you can keep your questions to yourself for now. Let's take care of her, not pester her."

"We'll be having questions for you, too, lass," one big man said. "You look ready for a Renaissance Faire, not a mountain climb."

"Made for lively conversation on our hike here," another firefighter said.

"Listen, all of you," Maolan said, her voice stern and loud. "Like I told you in the night, it's important no one know she's here or the blighters who did this just might come to finish the job."

The group stood silent, faces suddenly stern. "She's safe with us," the paramedic said. He placed a hand on Kidwell's head. "She's one of our own now."

Kidwell raised her free hand, pointing toward the group. A string or words flowed through her mind, but the morphine and her injured weakness blocked them from expression. "Later, guys," was all she said.

"Words of wisdom from the Prophet," another woman said, more teasing than critical.

"So be it, then," an older man said, one with the multiple bugles of a chief's insignia on his collar. "Let's get this job done."

They loaded and secured her efficiently into the Stokes Basket, tying her in with the soft but strong tubular webbing. As they did so, Kidwell was relieved she'd convinced Maolan to help her stumble to a far corner of the cave and empty her bladder before the arrival of the rescue squad. The chief himself took first turn as the anchor at the back of the cage, securely placing the harness over his shoulder and back while also grasping the cage firmly with both hands. The man in front placed his loop of webbing over one shoulder where it could be slipped away easily. Two firefighters on each side also grasped the handholds. Kidwell knew that if anything started to go wrong, they would all put the basket to the ground as gently as possible, and it would be the anchor's job to serve as the brake, especially if there was a steep incline.

As they stepped outside of the cave and onto the overhang just outside, Kidwell got her first glimpse of the landscape around and the village below. The mountain with the cave was little more than a hill compared to the Rocky Mountains of her home in New Mexico, but it was grand all the same. The lush green of the countryside took her breath away. Even in the distance the village was so beautiful, with a church at its center and scattering of stone buildings and shops, and whole neighborhoods of bright white cottages.

What a lovely place to be stranded. She didn't think much else for the rest of the journey as the gentle rocking of the basket and the comfort of the drug lulled her to sleep.

Chapter Eight

Overdue

"What do you mean you have no idea?" Aisha demanded, glaring at the phone resting in her hand, the speaker activated so she and Greg could both hear.

There was a momentary delay as the message traveled across thousands of miles. "Aisha, I am so sorry, but I know nothing. Kidwell never arrived at my office," Roberto answered from his office in The Hague.

Aisha swore softly in Arabic while Greg rocked anxiously back and forth on each foot. "Why did you ask her to do this? Don't you know what she means to so many people, to the world?" Her voice shook with emotion.

"To us," Greg mumbled.

"I know," Roberto answered. Even over the distance, they could hear his voice husky with emotion. "I'm worried sick too. *Ella es una amiga de mí corazon tambien.*"

Greg's cell phone rang. He stepped away as he looked at the Caller ID.

"Hey, Martin. Have you heard anything?" Greg asked into the phone.

"No. I was hoping you had," Martin responded.

"We're on the phone with Roberto now."

Greg heard Martin take a deep breath. "Greg,

I went to the fairy throne this morning with sage. I prayed and meditated."

"And?"

"Greg, she's alive. I know it," Martin answered.

Greg opened his mouth to respond when he heard his wife's phone beep.

"Allah, no!" Aisha said as she looked at the screen of her phone.

"What is it?" Greg, Roberto, and Martin asked in unison. "I'll call you back in a few," Greg said to Martin before pressing End on his phone.

Aisha's face was pale. "Not what, who," she answered. "I'll call back," she told Roberto, ending his call and answering the second. "Hello, Anna," she said, a protective and hesitant note in her voice. She kept the phone on speaker.

"Hello, Aisha. It's really good to hear your voice," Anna answered. "Is Greg there?"

Greg stepped closer to the phone. "I'm here."

"I...I miss you both. How are you?"

Aisha looked at Greg, and silently they shared confusion as to how to answer. "We're well enough," Greg said. He mouthed the words "Should we tell her?" to Aisha. She shrugged in answer.

"I called to pass along an important message," Anna said.

A thousand thoughts ran through Aisha's mind. Had Kidwell contacted Anna? Was Anna involved in her disappearance?

"Yes?" was all Aisha said.

"I don't know what happened but, well, an angel came to tell me that Kidwell was alive but hurt. That's all I know."

"How bad?" Greg demanded.

"I asked, but he wouldn't tell me. Aisha, Greg, what's happened?"

The couple looked at each other, confused. After a long pause, Aisha answered. "Anna, I'm not comfortable sharing that with you."

The subtle hum of the silent cell line could be heard during another long pause. Anna's voice was tight and restrained when she finally spoke.

"I understand. Please, please, take care of her."

"I promise, Anna. We'll do everything we can," Greg said.

"Well, then, I guess that's goodbye," Anna responded. "It truly was good to hear your voices."

Tears teased at Aisha's eyes, and her voice gentled. "It was good to talk with you, too, Anna." She chewed gently at her lower lip. "Are you well?"

"I'm growing. I'm healing."

"We were really surprised to learn you were living with Celia's family," Greg said. "I take it you two stayed together."

"No!" Anna nearly shouted. "That was the biggest mistake of my life. Surely you know that."

"We knew it," Aisha said. "We just didn't know if you knew it."

"But you're with her family—"

"They took me in. They aren't like her, Greg. I feel like a daughter here, and Celia was asked to leave."

"You're kidding," Aisha said.

"No. She's definitely the bad apple, and they don't know what to do with her."

"I know what I'd like to do with her," Greg said in a bitter voice.

Anna laughed with little humor. "You and her brothers should compare notes."

"Maybe we will one day," he responded.

"Anna, thank you for letting us know, about the angel that is," Aisha said.

"I pray with all my heart she's okay," Anna said.

"So do we," Aisha said.

The call ended with simple goodbyes. Aisha and Greg opened the screens on their phones, preparing to return Roberto and Martin's calls, ready to share the somewhat good news. They froze as Morris, the feline male who now served as Greg's combat instructor, stepped into the living room from the studio. He looked incongruous in the modern living room, dressed in a forest green tunic with a leather overlay along with black tights and high-topped boots. A sword was strapped to his back. Greg had never seen him without it.

"Why, might I ask, have you two stopped answering your paintings?" Morris asked, obviously peeved.

"What?" Aisha asked.

"Masat has been trying to reach you. She says she watched Kidwell be attacked. I understood she was looking through a mini-eye portal. Maolan jumped through the portal so suddenly it knocked Masat and her daughter down. Do you know what kind of force it takes to knock down a dragon?"

Aisha and Greg stood with mouths gaping. "I totally forgot about the dragon eye pendent," Greg said.

"Me too." Aisha slapped her palm against her forehead. "How could I forget? I painted it."

"What happened?" Greg demanded.

"Masat contacted me, asking me to come get you. Ask her yourself." Morris motioned toward the studio and the portal paintings.

They started for the studio when Aisha's phone rang. Aisha looked at the Caller ID, confused. "International," she said to Greg before answering.

"And a fine good morning to ya," a lilting voice said, sporting a heavy Irish brogue. "Would this be the lovely Aisha Sudda?"

Aisha rolled her eyes. *Telemarketer.* "Yes, it is," she answered coldly.

"Well now, this is Shamus Crowton from the village of Greenfields in County Tyrone, Northern Ireland, and I have a message from a couple of dear friends of yours."

Aisha's attitude changed abruptly, and she switched to speaker phone.

"Friends of ours, you say?"

"Aye. They be visiting our lovely village and wanted you to know it's a fine spot for rest and recovery for your friend who has had such a trying time with the work she does."

"Is she...Is she all right?" Greg asked.

"And this would be Mr. Greg Svenson, whom your friends speak of so highly?"

"That's me," Greg answered.

"Both your friends be doing fine, and the one is mending nicely from her woes, but they plan to stay a bit, give her a chance to get her feet under her so to speak."

"Yes," Aisha said. "We were worried because she was overdue."

"Aye, she said as much. She asked me to call because there are complications not allowing her to contact you directly right now."

"We understand," Greg said.

"She apologized for her change in plans, but she ran into a wee bit of trouble and was pleased when your other friend, one of our own Irish lasses, turned up out of the blue to give her a boost. They both decided a visit to her old Irish home was exactly what they needed, so here they are, and we're pleased to have 'em."

"Thank you so much," Aisha said.

"Our pleasure," he answered. "We're all grand fans of her book. Bye for now, and I hope you'll visit us one day." He paused. "Not sure your friends are up to company just yet, though."

"Thank you again," Aisha said.

"We're very grateful you called," Greg added just before the line went dead.

Morris leaned against the wall, tapping his fingers impatiently on the mantel. Greg looked at his arms master, then handed his phone to Aisha.

"You make the calls," he said. "I'll answer the painting."

Chapter Nine

Hard Work and Family

Anna worked side by side with Señora Martinez's sons, Emilio and Lucas. She felt nothing but joy when she climbed into the saddle of the blaze-faced bay gelding the two men had deemed gentle enough for her. Neither man had hidden their surprise when she actually proved to be a worthy hand as they rode through the high summer pasture gathering cows and calves and gently pushing them down the mountain. It was a little early for the move to lowland winter grazing, but Lucas had other work on the ranch where he was now foreman, and they would need to wean, brand, and vaccinate the calves before moving the herd to winter grazing. There was also the unpleasant task of castrating the young bulls, best done before the onset of winter. Neither of the Martinez brothers seemed concerned about any cattle missed in the heavy trees surrounding the mountain meadows, not even when the herd bull was among the missing.

"The cows and bull know the way," Emilio answered when Anna asked if she should return to look for them. "They'll find their way home in a day or two."

The day was long, begun with barely any daylight to guide them as the group rode into the mountains—the two Martinez brothers, Anna, and three of the hands from the Slant H Ranch where Lucas worked.

By the time they pushed the last of the herd into corrals, the light of evening had overlaid the softness filter over the light of the day. They settled the cattle into corrals where hay and water were already waiting before they turned to care for tired horses.

"You ride pretty fine for a lady," a Slant H hand said to Anna as they both unsaddled their mounts. His grin was full of cowboy charm despite being barely visible beneath his sandy mustache.

Anna sighed, gratified but sore and tired from the day's ride. It had been too long since her last trail ride with Kidwell. Her body remembered the skills, but the muscles had lost their familiarity with the saddle. The friendly cowboy worked as closely to her as he could throughout the day, and Anna knew she must deal with his kindly but unwanted attention.

"I have ridden most of my life," she answered. "As a child on my family's *rancho*." She paused, choosing her words. "Then for many years my wife and I rode the trails of the mountains."

The cowboy's smile petrified into a frosty expression. "Your…wife?"

Anna picked up her saddle, throwing it defiantly over her shoulder and holding it balanced on her back. "Yes, my wife," she said looking squarely at the cowboy, waiting to see his reaction, gauging if she would need to protect herself either verbally or physically. From her peripheral vision, she saw Emilio step out of the tack room where he had just deposited his saddle and bridle. He stood staring at the cowboy, waiting, and Anna knew she was not alone.

The smile returned, although subtly altered. "Well, goll-darn it! Guess I won't be asking you to go dancing this Saturday after all," he said.

Anna laughed, turning toward the tack room. "I'd say that's a safe guess."

"*¿Esta bien, hermana?*" Emilio asked softly as Anna passed.

"*Sí, bien.*" She blinked back tears and turned so that Emilio would not see them. She was deeply touched, not just by his concern, but even more so that he had called her "sister."

Horses were soon brushed, watered, and put away, the Martinez horses in the barn and the Slant H horses back in the trailer that would return them to the ranch.

Abuela Martinez and Emilio's wife had tables set in the yard beside the house, and they relayed platters of enchiladas (both green and red), ensaladas, sopapillas, and more from the house to the outdoor feast. As an added reward for the workers there was a washtub filled with ice and a smattering of cans of soda, outnumbered substantially by bottles of Dos Equis and Corona. The *caballeros* descended on the food like locusts. Even Anna's manners were forgotten as she sated the hunger nurtured by a long day spent in the saddle. Conversation ceased as the cowhands ate a feast better than for a king, for it was the heavy, hearty food needed by those accustomed to hard work. They finished the meal by the hissing light of a propane lantern, and it was full dark by the time the Slant H hands drove away, leaving their foreman behind. Lucas would spend the night in the main house, sleeping in the room he had once shared with Emilio and their other brother Antonio, who was now a teacher in the Albuquerque school system. In the morning, they would separate the calves to be weaned, branded, and castrated. It would be a different kind of hard work the following day.

Anna began gathering dishes from the table, preparing to return them to the kitchen.

"No, *Hita*," the grandmother said. "You have worked with the men today. Lupe and I will clean up from the meal."

Anna shook her head gently. "Abuela, you look tired too. I will at least help return everything to the house."

The older woman did not argue, a sign of the exhaustion Anna could see. Working together, it didn't take long for the outdoor dining room to be cleared and removed. When they started on dishes, it was Lupe who shooed Anna away.

"Go, rest, Anna." Lupe said. "My husband says you worked better than most men today, and you will need rest before tomorrow."

Anna did not argue, a sign of her own exhaustion. Sleep threatened to overcome Anna as she showered in the tiny bathroom the Martinez boys had built for her beside the barn bedroom she had claimed for herself. She collapsed on the old but comfortable bed, barely hearing the bawling of restless cattle in the nearby pens. Exhaustion trumped the outside cacophony. It took only minutes for Anna to welcome the darkness of sleep. As tired as she was, she still found the energy for her nightly ritual.

Heal her. Protect her, Anna prayed silently. Her last conscious thought was of Kidwell.

᪥᪥᪥᪥

Emilio was right—the bull and cows knew their way home. Still groggy from a sound sleep, Anna stepped out the door of her cozy room to find an Angus bull nearly the size of a Volkswagen grazing just ten feet from her. The massive beast looked at her with lazy eyes, mooing as he turned to walk toward the corrals, leading his cadre of six escapist cows with their accompanying calves. Anna knew the plan and crossed to open the gate to a small pen, already waiting with hay and water for the prodigal bovines. The bull trotted directly to the water trough, claiming a spot in the center as his wayward harem vied for positions to claim their own drink. They'd had a long walk from the mountain.

The day went well. As child and young woman Anna knew this job, having worked with her own family in the sorting of calves from cows, although it would always twist her heart to hear the plaintive bawling of mammas and babies separated for the inevitable weaning. The Martinez herd was small compared to the Slant H and other nearby spreads, mostly owned by the absentee wealthy, proud to brag of their wild west ranches and worked by cowhands who lived and preserved a still romantic lifestyle. Most of those cowboys lived as their fathers, grandfathers, and great-grandfathers had. It was an odd symbiosis shared by those who loved the life in different ways: the poor, rich in tradition and ancestral skills; and the wealthy, impoverished in skills and tradition but wealthy in the financial resources needed to preserve large-scale ranching.

In the end, thirty calves were ready to wean and process. Anna, working with Emilio's young son Ernesto, pushed calves up the alley and into the narrow feeder ending in the branding squeeze chute while Emilio and Lucas worked with well-practiced efficiency branding, vaccinating, and, when needed, castrating. Anna watched the bucket of cold water where the brothers tossed the raw sweetbreads. She suspected a family meal of "mountain oysters" would be on the menu sometime soon. The thought did not trouble her. She was a woman of the land, comfortable with the realities of that life.

It wasn't yet noon when she pushed the last three calves into the chute, finding herself looking forward to a lunch of leftovers and a bottle of cold Corona. That's when things changed.

A battered gray car pulled into the compound and parked beside the old trailer that had belonged to Emilio and Lucas's uncle.

"*Madre de Dios,* not her again," Emilio mumbled so low that Anna barely heard him over the complaining calves.

Anna understood. Her heart sank as she recognized Celia's car, somewhat more battered than the last time she'd seen it—the left rear fender bashed and the back bumper missing. As Celia stepped from the vehicle, Anna observed that both the car and its owner had seen better times. Celia was thin and moved with quick, jerky movements as she stepped from the vehicle. Anna had trouble reconciling this woman with the gentle creature she'd watch handle horses with such a loving and peaceful touch.

Celia walked to the corrals, hitching up her now too-large jeans and smoothing at her wrinkled shirt. She stepped onto the bottom rail and leaned across the fence.

"*Hola, hermanos.*" She laughed nervously. "Did you miss me?" She sniffed repeatedly. Her eyes were bloodshot, and there was a frenzied energy to her.

Cocaine, Anna thought. She leaned down and whispered to Ernesto. "Go quietly behind the barn and to your mother in the house." The boy eased away, doing as he was told.

"What do you want, Celia?" Emilio asked.

"Ah, *hermano grande.* You hurt me. Can't a woman just want to come home for a visit?"

"Haven't you hurt our mother enough?"

Lucas stared at his boots. "She prays for you," he said.

"What good does that do?" Celia said, spitting in the dirt to accent her words.

Normally a patient and quiet man, Lucas looked up, a spark of fire in his eyes. "I have wondered the same thing."

In that instant, Anna saw the strength and power that made the middle Martinez son a respected foreman on a large ranch. She had secretly doubted such a gentle soul could oversee such a grand undertaking.

Celia turned her attention to Anna. Her face contorted into a hatred that shocked Anna.

"You're still here?" Celia said, more of a statement than a question. "I take it my mama prefers you as a daughter."

That's when Anna smelled it: evil. Only once before had she known such a stench, smelled more with the soul than the nose. She looked deeply into Celia's eyes and realized the woman she'd known was no longer in control, if she ever truly had been.

"Yes, Celia, I'm still here, and I would gladly claim your mother as my own. She is a fine woman."

"You," Celia said, the anger apparent in her voice. "You robbed me of everything!" She jumped the fence with an almost inhuman leap and rushed across the corral, tripping over milling calves. "I hate you."

Anna held the horsewhip she'd used, snapping

behind the calves as she pushed them into the alley. Almost as reflex, when Celia was nearly upon her, she lashed out. As the thong of the whip connected with Celia's neck, the attacker cried out in pain, stopping her forward rush and hissing at Anna like an angry snake. Celia reached into her pocket, and a knife appeared in her hand. She extended the three-inch locking blade with a seamless flick of her thumb. Anna lashed with the whip again, but Celia lunged. Anna stopped the blade with the long handle of the whip, the blade slicing halfway through the flexible fiberglass interior. Anna grabbed for Celia's wrist, but Celia twisted free, swinging the blade toward Anna. Anna jumped back, the tip of the blade just catching her left forearm, leaving a long but shallow cut.

Emilio and Lucas tackled their sister simultaneously from behind, winding the woman and knocking the knife from her hand. They lay upon her, leaving her unable to move. Soundless at first, she finally regained her breath and began spewing a string of curses, first in a mix of Spanish and English, and then in a guttural, vile language none of them knew. The very sound filled Anna with a cold fear.

And then Señora Martinez was there, kneeling in the dirt and manure of the corral, weeping.

"*Mí nina. ¿Que haces?*" she asked, crying. "What have you done? What have you become?"

Anna knelt beside the older woman, fearful what the trauma could do to this woman she loved as a mother. She placed her arms around the abuela.

"Please, Abuela, go to the house. We will deal with her," Anna said.

She felt the older woman gather strength so intense Anna could feel the energy exuding from her.

"No," the old woman said. She stood slowly, dusting at her knees and leaning on Anna's shoulder as she regained her feet. Her voice was strong again as she spoke, taking charge. "Emilo, Lucas, keep her down. Anna, go to the barn and bring a rope."

Lupe called from the other side of the fence. "Should I call the sheriff?"

"No," the abuela said. She looked at her three children struggling in the dirt. "My sons, your sister is a *bruja* now. The law cannot help." She turned to Anna. "Get the rope. We must bind her as we prepare."

Anna dropped the whip and ran, climbing the fence without bothering for a gate. She grabbed a catch rope from the tack room and ran just as rapidly back to the corral. Working together, the two brothers and Anna were able to wrap the terrifying creature— hardly even appearing as a woman now—and securely bind her with the rope. What had once been Celia did manage a nasty bite on Emilio's hand. Anna grasped her by the hair while Lucas forced her jaw open, even punching her in the face before she finally released Emilio, spitting a chunk of his flesh into the dirt as she did so.

The abuela grabbed her son's hand, studying the wound. "Go to the house," she said. "Have Lupe wash it thoroughly with soap and water then cleanse it with holy water before binding it." She paused. "You know the jar with dirt from the *Santuario de Chimayo?*"

"*Sí, Mamma.*"

"Don't put it in the wound but spread it on the flesh around the wound." The old woman walked to the corral fence where Lupe waited. She whispered to her daughter-in-law. "After you have cared for your husband, there is a bag of salt in the kitchen cabinet.

Bring it to me."

"*Sí, Mamma Sophia.*"

Lucas, Anna, and Señora Martinez stood in a circle around Celia, who had finally gone quiet. She stared with hatred at the people she had once loved, and there was a sickening red glow to her eyes.

"Lucas, use your bandana to gag her so that she cannot bite again."

Carefully, the man did as his mother instructed. Celia snapped her teeth at him as he approached from behind, but she could not reach him, and he was able to secure the cloth in her mouth and tie it behind her head.

"Do you two think you can carry her to your uncle's trailer?" the old woman asked.

"*Mamma*, is it right for us to treat our sister—"

"Lucas, *hito*." She motioned toward Anna with her chin. "Can't you see she came here to kill Anna? If we release her, that is what will happen." Tears teased at her eyes. "And this is the only chance we have to save your sister—if she is still there."

Anna felt a cold certainty that the old woman was right. "Lucas, I think we can carry her." The man nodded in agreement.

They rolled Celia unceremoniously onto her stomach. Lucas lifted her by a strap of the rope where it coiled across her back, and Anna did the same on the rope around her legs. Celia struggled at first, but she stopped after the second time they dropped her.

"Please don't drop me again," she said, her voice distorted by the bandanna. Anna didn't know whether to be relieved or disappointed that she recognized Celia's voice and not the horrific sounds she'd made earlier.

Although Anna and Lucas were both winded and sweating when they finally got Celia inside the old single-wide trailer, the rest of the journey was uneventful. They laid their burden on the bed, and Anna's heart nearly broke when she saw the tears streaming down Celia's face. Working carefully, Lucas stepped behind his sister, untying the knot on the bandana and jumping away when the cloth came free.

"Please, brother, please," Celia said.

Lucas stepped in her direction, reaching for a knot in the rope.

"Stop," the abuela demanded. "As soon as she is free, Celia will be gone and another will take her place." She grabbed her son by one arm and Anna by another, guiding them forcefully out the door.

"*Mamma*, those ropes will not hold her for long. She will wiggle free," Lucas said.

"It will not matter." She turned to Lupe and Emilio as they walked toward them, Lupe caring a five-pound bag of picking salt. The abuela took the bag, opening a small corner at the top so that a thin stream of salt could escape. The others watched and followed as she dribbled salt just outside the trailer.

"She cannot leave now," the old woman said as she joined the line of salt into a full circle.

"Will it hold her?" Anna asked.

"The salt and our faith will hold her."

The orders continued. She sent Emilio, Lupe, and Ernesto to town for a doctor to care for Emilio's hand and for Ernesto to be left with cousins. Lucas was sent to finish branding the calves.

Señora Martinez turned to Anna, placing a gentle hand on her shoulder. "You and I, we have very special work to do."

Chapter Ten

Intercession

It was the hardest work she'd ever known. Side by side, the abuela and Anna prayed. Through the afternoon and into the evening they prayed. At first her knees and back complained, yet Anna prayed. The old woman beside her held her rosary like a lifeline as together they knelt before a niche, home to a *santo* of Our Lady of Guadalupe, one carved and painted by the Señora's late husband.

Anna had followed the old woman's lead as they entered the old adobe home, leaving her sons and daughter-in-law to their individual tasks. As the old woman turned out electric lights, closed curtains and shades darkening the house, Anna followed suit, leaving most of the house in darkness. Only the main room had light from the flicker of the forty or fifty candles they had ignited.

As she worked in the back of the house shutting down lights and closing windows, Anna heard the muffled sounds as the abuela made a phone call, speaking in rapid Spanish too far away for Anna to understand the conversation. She took the moment to make her own call, pulling a cell phone from her pocket. Tears trickled unbidden down her face as she punched the listing for a contact she had not dared to call for many months. Her breath came in fits and spurts as she listened to the ring.

"Hello, Anna?" a voice answered, hesitant and guarded.

"Martin," she said. "It is so, so good to hear your voice."

There was a long pause. "It's good to hear yours as well," the young Apache answered.

"Martin, I know I made a horrible mistake." She wiped at her tears with the back of her hand. "I understand that you may never trust me again but know that I still love you as a son, and my heart is broken that I have lost your love."

"Anna." She heard his voice break with emotion. "You never lost my love, only my trust."

A sob temporarily robbed Anna of the power of speech. "I know. I lost faith in myself as well." She took a deep breath, gathering her strength. "But I am finding it again, Martin."

"Anna, why have you called? Kidwell is not here."

"I know. I called for you."

"Why?"

"Martin, dear boy, you have a strength and soul that is rare. You have trained to be a shaman, and you are one, whether or not you know it yet."

Martin laughed gently. "Kidwell says never to trust anyone who calls themselves by that title."

"And you don't, but I do." Anna licked dry lips, tasting the dust from the morning's work. She'd almost forgotten. It felt like another lifetime. "Martin, we need you. We need a shaman."

"I awoke this morning knowing someone would call. I went to water, bathed, and prayed through the morning. The spirits spoke, helping to center my soul. Who is it who needs me?"

"The Martinez family."

The silence on the other line was so intense Anna could hear the pulse beating in her ears. "Celia's family?" Martin finally asked.

"Yes."

"Aisha and Greg said you were living there. They said Celia was gone."

"She's back, Martin."

"That is not good."

Anna laughed bitterly. "That is an understatement. Martin, remember the Dark One, the man-slash-monster Kidwell fought?"

"Need you ask? Who could forget?"

"Martin, Celia came back, but it's not Celia. It's like…well, like him."

Martin mumbled something in Apache. Anna didn't know the words, but she knew it was a prayer. "I will come," he finally answered. "Is it at the Martinez *Rancho*?"

"Yes. Martin, bring sage and sweet grass."

"I will."

The line disconnected unceremoniously.

Neither woman spoke as they came together in the main room. The old woman handed Anna an embroidered pillow. The abuela knelt on her own pillow, already in place and indented perfectly for her knees, knees that had spent many hours on that pillow, much of which had been in supplication for the same daughter for whom she prayed now.

At first, there were words to Anna's prayers, some mumbled, some thought, but words nonetheless. In time they faded away, as did her awareness of the discomfort of knees, back, and even arms where she rested them on the rough wood of the kneeling stand.

She had seen Kidwell, and even Martin, reach states of deep prayer. Today, she finally knew it herself. The energy of air and light was real for her, felt as clearly as a cool breeze, not just against her skin, but her very soul. With her eyes closed, she did not see them, but she was acutely aware of companions in the room, and she knew without words that she and the abuela did not fight this battle alone. She was not entirely sure if the beings were of body or light or a combination of both. At one point, a bright light penetrated her closed eyelids, and she felt the warmth of a hand on her shoulder. She looked to see the angel who had visited her before, shining with a golden light. He nodded support, and she nodded in return before returning to the deep, soulful and somewhat mindless state of her prayers. Only once during their hours of prayer had Anna risen, responding to a desperate bodily need to urinate. After, she paused in the kitchen to drink deeply from sweet water and fill a water bottle which she took with her to the main room. She was gentle as she touched the old woman, insisting that she drink and helping her up so that she, too, could deal with baser bodily needs. Within moments after kneeling again both women were lost in the netherworld of deep meditation.

Anna had no idea how long she journeyed in that world of visions and emotions, of complex clarity beyond the mind. A gentle voice finally brought her back to the physical world.

"It is time."

Anna opened her eyes and turned stiffly to see an elderly priest looking at her, his body bent with age but his eyes shining with a youthful light. Padre Francisco; Anna knew him without being told. Señora Martinez had spoken of him many times, and she felt certain she knew whom the abuela called. As she became aware of her surroundings, she breathed in the distinctive odor of burning sage and sweetgrass, and she turned to see Martin seated cross-legged behind her, the traditional purifying incense of indigenous people smoldering in an earthen bowl before him. He rose in a fluid motion, offering his hands to the elderly priest and to Anna, helping them rise and then doing the same for the old woman.

There was no sense of time for Anna in that moment. She knew the light of day had been replaced by darkness, but nothing more. Despite the continued dissociative feeling, Anna's heart sang with joy at the sight of the young Apache.

"Hello, *shamaa*," he said.

Anna wept. He'd called her "mother." He stepped to her, wrapping her in a strong embrace, which she gratefully returned.

"It is time," the old priest repeated.

Martin picked up his incense bowl and a painted feather fan resting on the floor beside the bowl. First with Anna, then the abuela, and finally, even the priest, Martin smudged them, purifying their energy before they faced true evil. Holding the smoke before him, Martin started above their heads, waving the fan to push smoke down to their feet, then back up, finally waving a vigorous "X" in the air above them, dissipating any negativity. Anna raised her hands before her and automatically turned clockwise so that Martin could repeat the exercise on her back. Señora Martinez followed Anna's cue as Martin smudged the old woman. He paused before the priest until the old holy man smiled and nodded his agreement.

The priest turned to a table where he'd laid out a rich purple altar cloth. He retrieved objects he had laid there—a cross, a vial of holy water, and a small incense burner hanging from a chain and already exuding the gentle smoke of incense. Martin gathered his earthen bowl then scattered more sage and sweetgrass over the coal that smoldered within. He retrieved from the table a leather bag, one Anna recognized as the one he used to carry sacred materials, and he hung it crosswise on his body by a long, woven leather cord. Señora Martinez carried only her rosary.

You need sage, a voice said in Anna's head. *Two bundles.* Anna turned to Martin and opened her mouth to speak, but he beat her to it.

"I heard," he said as he reached into his bag to retrieve two smudge sticks which he lit from the coal in the bowl and then blew into smoldering light before handing them to Anna. As she watched, Anna remembered he had long been the fire keeper for many a ceremony for both the Apache and his relatives among the Diné.

The priest led the small procession out into the darkening evening light. As soon as they left the house, Anna could hear bangs and growls from within the single-wide trailer where they had left Celia, or whoever that being was now. Emilio and Lucas sat in lawn chairs they had placed between the trailer and the main adobe home. A lever-action rifle lay across Emilio's lap, and a pistol rested in a holster on Lucas's belt. Anna felt great comfort in knowing they had been their guardians during the long prayers. Both men stood as they saw the procession leave the house.

"What has happened, *hitos*?" the abuela asked.

"You were right, *Mamma*. The salt kept the beast

inside," Emilio answered. "She threw the door open once but acted as though she'd been burned when she reached the line of salt. She hasn't tried to come outside since, but the sounds...*Madre de Dios*, the sounds have been horrible."

Anna stepped beside Lucas. She looked pointedly at the pistol on his belt. "You would be willing to kill your sister?"

Lucas looked at her with tired eyes. "If I must. Besides, that's not my sister."

"I will go in first," the priest said. "You boys must stay here. You have guarded us well." He turned to Anna and Martin. "I will need warriors at my back, so you two must follow." Lastly, he faced the abuela. "My dear sister, do you wish to save your daughter?"

"*Sí, Padre, con todo mí corazon.*"

"Then go back to the niche. Pray to Our Lady. The prayers of a mother may be what is needed to save us all."

Señora Martinez looked at the old trailer with pain in her eyes, but she said nothing. She simply turned and walked with heavy steps back toward the house.

The old man, walking now as though thirty years had been shed from his body, turned and moved confidently toward the trailer, his head held high. Anna and Martin trotted to catch up with him, flanking the old man on each side but a step behind. When they arrived at the trailer, the door was still wide open, Anna assumed from when Celia had tried to leave before encountering the salt circle. The priest did not hesitate as he walked up the three short steps, the cross held before him, the incense burner swinging from its chain held in his other hand. All three held their "weapons," Anna with the sage and Martin with his smudge bowl and feather fan. As soon as the incense wafted into the trailer, they heard a horrific scream and a growl from the inside. Anna's heartbeat quickened, but the trio moved inside the structure undaunted. Anna was reminded of her days in the fire department, working alongside Kidwell and entering a structure fire. She felt the same sensation, all fear abating and a different part of her mind taking control, feeling as though everything moved rapidly and in slow motion at the same time.

It took a few moments for Anna's eyes to adjust to the dark interior of the trailer, but she could see a form cowering in the corner, behind one end of a ragged couch. It was Celia...sort of. The sounds emanating from the form were not human, and the eyes glowed red. The priest shifted the chain of the incense burner to the same hand that held the cross, and he pulled the vial of holy water from a pocket on his tunic, flipping the top free easily with one hand. He spoke in Latin, and while Anna could not understand the words, the meaning was clear. With authority, the holy man demanded that the woman be freed of her evil invader as he flung drops of holy water at the creature.

For all their hours of prayer and preparation, Anna was amazed at how quickly things happened. As soon as the holy water hit, Celia's body screamed then went silent, collapsing on the floor in a heap. Above her, two dark, shadowy figures hovered in the air. *Two. She was possessed by two,* Anna thought.

The priest called again in Latin, flinging holy water, then something happened Anna never would have dreamed possible. There was a wave of darkness, like a flash only in reverse, and the entire trailer was filled with a foul stench. Standing before them were no longer two dark shaped spirits, but two living, flesh-and-blood foul beasts. They each looked like gargoyles: hunched and dark with large heads, foul fangs dripping drool, heavily muscled bodies, arms and legs with long claws on both hands and feet. As though planned, Anna and Martin moved together to shoulder the priest back, forming a human shield before him. There was another flash, this time of light, and Anna found herself holding not two smudge sticks, but a round, metal shield held by leather loops over her left hand and arm, and a short sword clutched in her right. She had never held a sword or shield in her lifetime, but they felt oddly familiar, and her body knew how to use them. In her peripheral vision, she could see that Martin now held a wooden lance topped with a metal spear point, painted feathers hanging from the base of the spearhead. In his other hand he had a leather and wooden shield painted with a medicine wheel in bright colors. The two warriors faced off against the monsters before them. Formerly ready to attack, both beasts now growled hesitantly at the newly armed warriors.

While the beasts stood wary, the priest moved with a speed unexpected for his age. He lunged past Martin, falling to the floor and grasping at Celia's body then crawling rapidly backward, pulling her behind him. Martin moved quickly, shielding the priest from a blow with his shield and slashing at the demon's face with his lance. The second beast moved toward the priest, but stepped back again as Anna moved forward, her shield before her and her sword raised for a slashing blow. The priest dragged Celia rapidly across the floor and toward the door.

"Go!" Anna yelled at the holy man as she stepped

between him and the two demons.

After Martin's lance scoured a deep gash on the demon's face, the creature hissed in anger and lunged for the Apache. Martin parried the claws with his shield, and the leather tore from the blow, leaving deep scratches in the wood beneath. Martin stabbed with his spear, the point finding home squarely in the middle of the demon's chest. Simultaneously, the creature screamed and there was an explosion of such force that Martin was thrown back hard against the wall, the outline of his shape in the drywall as he slid, stunned, to the floor. Anna stabbed at her demon and he countered the blade with his claws, taking a nasty cut on his arm but successfully pushing the blade so that she only achieved a glancing blow, cutting his side but not penetrating the ribs. Anna felt a jolt to her hand so hard that her fingers felt numb and the sword fell from her hand. She held the shield before her, looking into the snarling face of the demon, now just a foot away.

I shouldn't have called Martin, was her thought as she prepared to die.

Things changed so rapidly that Anna couldn't fully comprehend. A wavering heat haze formed in the middle of the room which coalesced into a shape that was effervescent black, a layer of rainbow over it, like a raven's wings.

"Harrana!" Anna screamed, not even knowing how she knew the name of the dragon now before her.

Run! She had no time to pause for comprehension, but she recognized Kidwell's voice. A stunned Martin had risen and was stumbling toward her, his cracked shield still hanging from his arm. Anna grabbed and dragged him behind her, toward the door. As they half fell through the door, she heard the dragon roar, and the entire room filled with fire—dragon fire. The screams of the demons were agony but lasted only briefly. She glanced toward the sky as she and Martin lay stunned and panting on the ground. She saw two dark, cloudlike shapes rush from the trailer and fly rapidly to the sky. *They're gone*, she thought. She saw Kidwell, the human Kidwell, stumble from the trailer and down the stairs. Kidwell collapsed to her knees after only a few steps away from the burning trailer. She knelt, her head thrown back and her face in a grimace of pain. She held a hand to her now bleeding shoulder, and she was dressed incongruously in a pair of flannel pajamas adorned with images of Celtic harps.

Martin recovered enough to stumble to Kidwell's side. "Kid," he called. "Are you all right?"

Kidwell smiled from a soot-streaked face and patted the hand of her young protector as he put a protective arm around her shoulder.

"I'll be okay," she said. She pointed with her chin, a habit she'd learned from her Apache friend, toward the two brothers as they scrambled to turn off propane and electricity and drag garden hoses from every hydrant on the place. In the distance, the sound of sirens could already be heard. "My son, help deal with the fire. I'll be okay."

Martin stood to do as he was bidden. As he left, Kidwell looked directly at Anna, and Anna feared her heart would either leap from her chest or stop beating entirely.

"Kidwell," Anna whispered. "How did you know?"

"An angel came for me," she answered. "And I heard the voice of an old woman, praying for help."

Anna crossed to Kidwell, half walking and almost crawling. She put a hand tentatively to Kidwell's bleeding shoulder.

"You're hurt."

"Doctor Conner is going to be very upset with me," Kidwell answered, laughing with little humor. A worried crease appeared on her forehead. "Maolan may kill me."

"Who?" Anna asked.

"Never mind."

Anna's hand moved from the shoulder to the back of Kidwell's head. Both women leaned forward, their foreheads touching.

"I have missed you," Anna said.

"And I've missed you," Kidwell answered.

The kiss was as natural and inevitable as a thirsty man gulping water. Tears streaked down both their now dirty faces. It was brief. Kidwell turned her face away.

"Anna," she said, pain obvious in her voice. "I…I cannot risk failure again." She looked into Anna eyes and gently stroked her cheek. "I cannot risk you."

Kidwell stood unsteadily. As Anna watched, the air around Kidwell took on a heat-haze look. For a moment there was a flash of effervescent black, then Kidwell simply disappeared.

Anna sobbed. She wondered if she could survive her heart breaking all over again. She only became aware of the world around her when Martin knelt at her side, wrapping her in strong arms.

"She came for us when we needed her," he said. He grasped her head and held it to his shoulder. "She will always love you, even if she cannot be with you."

Anna pushed him gently away, her attention

drawn by the arriving fire trucks.

"We need to move. We're in the way," she said.

Martin helped her to her feet and led her to the yard in front of the main house. The elderly priest and the *abuela* sat in the two chairs the men had brought to the yard. The priest sat with a blanket around his shoulders, a water bottle in his hand. He very much looked his age.

Celia sat on the ground in front her mother, crying inconsolably into her mother's lap.

"I'm so sorry, *Mamma*," she said repeatedly, the voice sounding like a young child. Anna wondered if that had been the last time she had truly been Celia, alone without a demon companion.

ଈୈଈୈ

None of the people below noticed the rustling in the treetops, some yards from where the group huddled around the old woman and her prodigal daughter. Two figures hunched together, perched on the same branch, resembling a pair of oversized vultures. Upon closer inspection, if one knew where to look, they would see clearly not vultures but two living gargoyles, misplaced from ancient battlements.

One figure leaned close, whispering in the other's ear. "What should we report?"

"What we saw," the other answered. "Another minion has failed to destroy either the rider or the dragon."

The first gargoyle looked every direction nervously before again leaning to his companion, whispering ever so softly. "I'm glad."

Surprised, the second figure repeated his

companion's guilty search for any listener. "Me too." He finally mouthed the words, not daring to give them sound. He reached inside the pocket of the dragon-leather vest, the only clothing he had ever owned. His fingers sought and fondled a stone amulet, the rough figure of a full-bodied goddess, one given him by their Governess not long after she'd been recruited to the demon world, when she still bore a semblance of her dark, human beauty. At least the figure had once resembled a goddess. Millennia of secret fondling by the gargoyle had worn away the stone, leaving only an indistinct shape. The two gargoyles were not alone, secretly pleased at their banishment from the hellish universe that was their ancestral home. Like so many, they sought those tasks far from the Governor's eyes, observing the Earth and the living creatures dwelling there, especially the species with the greatest promise for both good and evil: humans.

The first gargoyle rocked from one foot to the other, untroubled by the great distance between ground and limb. His companion looked at him, noting the damp streaming down the other's cheeks.

"Don't let the Governor see those tears," he warned.

Wiping roughly at the damp, he continued to cry as he watched the humans below. "Pug, what is it like to love, to be loved?"

"I don't know," the gargoyle responded, fingering the stone. *But I wish I did.*

Chapter Eleven

Respite

Maolan had forgiven Kidwell, more or less. No permanent damage had been done to Kidwell's injured shoulder, although the medical staff and Maolan were deeply concerned at Kidwell's brush with shock after she'd teleported back to her hospital room, drained by battle and two teleportations. Maolan had been tightlipped and silent when Kidwell reappeared. During her unexplained absence, the auburn-haired woman paced impatiently as she and the nurses struggled to understand the disappearance. When her lover abruptly appeared, lying on the floor, too exhausted to even stand, Maolan lifted her to the bed, silently horrified at the cold Kidwell's skin exuded through the thin, soot-covered pajamas.

"Where did you go?" the Celtic woman demanded, gentle despite her anger and concern. She felt the frailty of the normally strong woman she held. Maolan's mouth felt cottony dry with fear.

"I had to," Kidwell answered. She touched Maolan's cheek. "Later, dearest. When I'm stronger."

The head nurse pushed Maolan aside, directing a look at the warrior woman so stern even Maolan was intimidated.

"Out," the nurse commanded Maolan, then turned to bark orders to another nurse. Maolan stepped into the hallway, trusting the healers within the room, but she watched, silent and stern. The doctor arrived, and things happened quickly. In short order, they had the Prophet warmed, stabilized, and rebandaged. An IV bag hung beside the hospital bed, dripping what Maolan comprehended as life-giving fluid and medications but had no clue as to the specifics. Kidwell fell into a heavy sleep. When the crisis was over, the medical team left, and Maolan returned to the room. The once stern nurse brought a cot and bedding, unfolding and making the tiny bed without saying a word. Maolan slept fitfully, but she would not have slept at all had she returned to the cozy room above a nearby pub that the mayor had arranged for her.

By the next morning Kidwell was herself again, barely allowing Maolan to place a protective arm around her as she shuffled from bed to the bathroom, or "toilet," as the Irish staff so frequently reminded her. When breakfast arrived—a full one including two soft-boiled eggs and wonderful bacon serendipitously shaped like a meaty map of Great Britain—neither Maolan's wrath nor curiosity could wait any longer.

"And what be ye thinking last night?" she demanded as Kidwell scooped up the last of her egg, following it with a hearty bite of toast with jam. "Ye could have died, silly woman. Then where would we all be?" Rose-red spots appeared on Maolan's cheeks, a sure indication of her anger.

Kidwell halted mid-chew, glancing guiltily at her friend and lover. She renewed chewing, rapidly washing it all down with a drink from the ubiquitous cuppa' tea on her tray. She looked at Maolan. The Celt was no longer in armor of leather, bronze and iron, but she could instill respect and fear even dressed in modern jeans, T-shirt, and simple short boots. She needed no armor nor sword for anyone to know she was a warrior.

"I had to go," Kidwell responded. "An angel came for me."

Maolan's eyes widened. Some of the anger evaporated, and her face softened to reflect less anger and more of the fear that was its source.

"Aye, those summonses are not to be ignored. But where and for whom?"

Kidwell replaced her cup to its saucer gently and placed her hand on top as if she thought it would fly right off the plate. Her shoulders rose and fell as she took a deep breath.

"In New Mexico." Another deep breath. "For Anna, the Martinez family and..." She hesitated. "And Celia.

The cup flew. Launched across the room to shatter against the wall, leaving a splot of tea against the light green paint. When a nurse stuck her head in the room at the sound, Kidwell gave her a warning look and motioned for her to close the door. The nurse obeyed.

"Careful, love. These aren't ancient times. Throwing crockery is not looked upon kindly these days," Kidwell said.

Maolan paced the full length of the tiny room. "Will those two women ever leave you alone? Us alone?" She reached for the plate, but Kidwell used her good hand to hold it as far as she could from the angry woman.

"No more crockery. Just yell at me. I won't break."

Tears filled her eyes as Maolan stepped to the

bedside, holding Kidwell's face gently between her hands. "You were last night, darlin'. Broken you were in a way I hadn't seen since...since—"

"Since I was dragon, in a lost battle."

"Aye," Maolan said, tears sliding gracefully from eye to chin. "I lost Falong then, and, in a different way, you and Annalome too." She swiped at the tear with the back of her hand. "I canna' bear the thought of that happening again, now that I have you back."

Kidwell patted the bed beside her uninjured side. "Come here," she said.

Maolan walked around the bed as Kidwell replaced the plate to the tray and pushed the rolling table to the side. The bed was not large, but they managed to make room for them both, and Maolan nestled comfortably into the tiny space, her body warm against her lover's and her head on Kidwell's shoulder. They both sighed a deep relief.

Abruptly, the door flung open. Standing in the doorway was the day shift head nurse glaring at them sternly—apparently, sternness was in the job description. In one hand she held a damp rag and a waste bin in the other.

"Well now," the woman said. "Sorry if I be disturbing the two of you, but it would seem we have a broken cup and a tea stain needing attention."

Maolan jumped from the bed. "Give me those. I broke it. I'll clean it up."

"Aye. You will," the nurse said, thrusting both objects into Maolan's hands. She turned tail, closing the door behind her. Only the pneumatics mechanisms of the door prevented it from slamming.

Kidwell and Maolan looked at each other and then laughed, only half-heartedly suppressing the sound of their humor. As Maolan cleaned, Kidwell described the events of the previous night.

☙ ☙ ☙ ☙

With confidence, Kidwell held the lines of the team pulling the pony cart. In a short time, both she and Maolan had grown to love the sturdy Irish ponies entrusted to them by one of the local farmers. Trained for both cart and saddle, the pair had been their ticket to exploring the mountains and valleys surrounding the village. When she'd first been released from the hospital, it had been all Kidwell could manage to spend a few hours each day sitting in one of the ancient wooden chairs in the garden beside the cottage which the affable mayor had arranged for them. He'd even offered the use of a car, but Kidwell could not yet drive and Maolan still viewed the horseless wagons as a magic she wasn't sure she could trust. The ponies and cart had been an even better answer, one they both preferred even after Kidwell was fit to drive.

"So, Maolan, my lass, you can't drive a motor car?" the mayor had asked. He removed his cap and scratched his bald pate, flashing an ageless smile at the two women. "Do you ride a horse? Can you drive a cart?"

Both women laughed. "Like it was second nature for us," Kidwell answered.

"Problem solved then," the mayor said.

The cottage was tiny, built in the sixteenth century, with deep stone walls and a thatched roof. The one bathroom held toilet, sink, and a clawfoot tub, one they'd both grown to love. All rested on a wooden floor four inches above the rest of the house's foundation, a necessity in the eventual retrofitting of a cottage built before indoor plumbing was even imagined. There were two tiny bedrooms with plain but starkly beautiful antique farm furniture. Once a week, a maid came to clean. If she noticed that only one bed was used, she said nothing. The first few days, women of the village brought food, more than they could possibly eat. They'd taken to inviting some of the folk back in the evening, sharing meals and tales. Maolan was fascinated to learn what had happened to the people of her homeland. Both women were amused that the cave overlooking the village was still known as the Dragon's Weyr.

Kidwell healed quickly. Within a few days, she and Maolan were exploring in the cart, Maolan driving and Kidwell sitting in the back wrapped in blankets and surrounded by pillows. At first she smiled in pleasure as Maolan fussed over her, but the pleasure soon wore thin. The independent woman wasn't comfortable being coddled. One morning Maolan awoke to find Kidwell gone from their bed. She went looking and found the still convalescing woman saddling one of the ponies, favoring only slightly her injured shoulder.

"So, how do you feel about a ride before breakfast?" Kidwell said.

Maolan nodded agreement, retrieving tack from the small stable, then catching and saddling her own pony. They'd ridden for only an hour, Maolan insisting she was hungry, an obvious ruse to hide her concern for the paleness of Kidwell's face.

By the time Kidwell was released from the hospital, Roberto from the World Court was certain no one knew Kidwell had been in the arms dealer's office. An agent of the Court made a "fishing trip" to

Ireland, retrieving the memory stick from Kidwell. They were no longer in hiding and had established cell phone and computer contact with Martin and Aisha and Greg, as well as Admiral O'Hare.

It was a honeymoon. At moments Kidwell felt guilty, wondering where she was needed in the world, or in any other world for that matter. Maolan eased her fears, reminding her that an injured and unfit Kidwell could be a hazard more than a help. In the narrow bed, not quite a Full by modern standards, the two finally had time to sort through the confusing complications of their relationship. When they had been the Four, in a sense Harrana and Maolan had been the least close of the quartet, but that was a relative comparison. Many beings never know the level of intimacy shared among all of the Four. Perhaps only a dragon and rider could comprehend that level of sharing of mind and soul, but they had bonded not as two but as four, sharing the mission as protectors of their clans, both human and dragon. As hatchlings, Harrana and Falong were soul-siblings from the very beginning, sharing adventures with their older sister Masat, the three building a close psychic bond. When the two dragons found their riders, the psychic bond jumped the normal boundaries so that all four shared not just thoughts but the very root of their hearts. When one cried, the others tasted tears; when one laughed, the mirth spread to four hearts. None of the four were surprised when Annalome and Maolan became lovers, although the deeply ingrained sibling bond made the possibility laughable for the two dragons. At some level, Kidwell knew that truth, although a still spotty memory hid the details from her.

"*A ghrá*, rest and heal in heart and soul as well

as body. Would do no one good to have you fall under the burden," Maolan said to Kidwell.

Kidwell listened. It was so easy to listen, lying in the dark, warm in the arms of a woman who was friend, sister, lover—the only person in the universe who could understand and touch her, body and soul, at the same level she had shared with Anna. When they made love, there was physical pleasure, but it was more mellow, more like a deep river than the flowing rapids of passion Kidwell had known in the early days with Anna. Sometimes, in the darkness, they shared a deep grief, Kidwell for her rider and Maolan for her dragon. At some level, they would always be the Four. They shared a bond no other beings in the universe would ever know nor truly understand.

This day, it was not the comforting softness of their Irish bed they shared, but the rough, wooden seat of an Irish pony cart. Off to the village for the day's shopping. They sat side by side laughing and talking, pointing out hawks and rabbits they saw along the way, waving at the village folk they'd come to know.

Their first trip to the village had been far different. It was only a few days after Kidwell was up and about, still slow in motion and easily tired. A cell phone and computer were at the top of her list, longing to hear the voices of Aisha, Greg, and Martin, and knowing she must write, preserve the lessons learned for the ongoing creation of *The Book of Kidwell*. Modern commerce was new to Maolan. Choices were limited in the village, but a town center shop had what was needed to fulfill their basic communication needs.

"I dunna' understand half of what's on these shelves," Maolan whispered to Kidwell.

"Time, dear. Give it time. You're learning your

way in this world."

At the cash register, Kidwell pulled a credit card from her wallet and laid it on the counter. The woman behind the register scanned the small laptop, cell phone, and prepaid cell minutes card before the amount showed on the keypad and Kidwell inserted the card in the slot.

"But where's the coin?" Maolan demanded.

Kidwell laughed. "In this card," she said just as the machine beeped, letting her know she could remove the card.

Maolan grabbed it from her hand and stared at the card. "Magic then?"

"In a sense. It's not real coin, just electronic messages that exchange money from my account to the store's."

"No gold? No silver? Is there no money exchanged?"

A man, apparently the owner, stepped up to the counter.

"Aye, money is exchanged," he said. "But the banks keep the records."

"So, there's coin in the bank?"

"Not exactly," Kidwell answered. "Most money is paper now."

"But how can the paper be worth anything? Isn't it just paper?"

"At one time the symbols on the paper represented the precious metals held by the government," Kidwell answered.

"What does it represent now?"

Kidwell, the clerk, and the store owner shared confused looks.

"Damnation." The man scratched his head.

"What does it represent?"

"I haven't a clue," Kidwell said.

The woman behind the counter laughed as she pulled a five-euro note from her pocket. "I'm going on break," she said, then looked directly at Maolan, waving the note in her direction. "And this, dearie, represents a cuppa' tea and a custard tart from the shop across the lane, plus some change in me pocket so I can do it again tomorrow."

Kidwell laughed, and Maolan looked confused. As they picked up their purchases and turned to leave, the shop owner spoke to Maolan.

"Lass," he said. "The young lads down pub say the sight of you gives them pleasant dreams, but I swear you'll be giving me nightmares this night. I own this shop, or do I? It's bought and paid for with money I never actually saw, and now I doubt if it really exists."

Kidwell grasped Maolan's hand and urged her toward the door. "Quick, let's go home before you destroy the economic security of the entire village."

And so they left, Kidwell resting in a nest of pillows and blankets in the back of the cart as the auburn-haired woman drove the team. Still healing, she was tired from the excursion but so looking forward to sharing with Aisha the tale of Maolan's first modern shopping experience.

❧❧❧❧❧

The dark of the night surrounded the cottage and the curtains at the window gently undulated under the power of a cool summer breeze. Kidwell lay awake, rolling from back to side as the tears flowing silently from the corners of her eyes and threatened to fill her ears. The dream had been so real. Anna stood beside a fast-moving stream, her gaze focused on Kidwell, a sad smile illuminating her face. Behind her were the steep mountains and Ponderosa pines of their New Mexico. Kidwell stood on the opposite bank, the green grass of Ireland below her feet. Anna raised her hand, reaching out tentatively, even sensually, as though she could will herself across the water. Despite the distance, Kidwell felt the gentle touch of Anna's fingers along the side of her face.

She awoke, lying perfectly still, listening to the steady breathing of the woman beside her. As Kidwell rolled to her side, she spooned around the shield maiden, burying her face in Maolan's sweet-smelling mane of auburn hair. *How can I love two women so deeply?* Kidwell's pain from the dream eased as she relaxed in the physical presence of her lover. The pitch and pace of Maolan's breathing changed, and Kidwell felt Maolan's subtle tensing as Maolan transitioned from sleep to wakefulness. The Celtic woman rolled toward her lover, moving to place an arm around Kidwell, and Kidwell eased naturally into the close embrace, her head on Maolan's shoulder.

"What troubles you, *A ghrá?*" Maolan asked.

"Just a dream."

Maolan lay silent, but only for a few moments. "Annalome?"

"Yes. I'm sorry, and I hope you know the depth of my feelings for you."

"I know," Maolan answered. "There can never be another bond like that between dragon and rider."

"Was it like this when you lost Falong?"

As Kidwell lay close, Maolan's very scent changed subtly. *Grief*, Kidwell thought. *She smells of grief.*

"Aye," Maolan answered.

"How long will this pain last?"

Maolan placed both arms around Kidwell and kissed her gently before nuzzling her neck then placing her mouth directly over Kidwell's ear.

"Forever," she whispered.

They kissed again and again. For the moment, their grief was forgotten.

Chapter Twelve

Meanwhile, At the Convent

An acolyte prayed alone in the small shrine, so deep in her prayers she barely noticed when the Mother Superior knelt beside her. Tears streamed down the young woman's face, eyes closed, a posture of supplication before the figure of Our Lady. Together they prayed for some time until the older nun touched the young woman's shoulder and spoke softly.

"It is time for your rest, Sister. You must be up early for prayers."

They both rose and walked silently from the shrine and across the courtyard to the convent. The Mother Superior spoke again, softly but clearly.

"Do you still pray for guidance?"

"Of course, Sister. I knew when I came here it was where I was supposed to be, but I do not feel it is where I am to stay. I have other work to do. I must make amends."

"What is that work?"

"I don't know." The young woman's voice was anguished. "That is the guidance I seek."

A dark figure, a hooded man, stepped from the shadows, startling the women.

"You must come with me," he said with an accent neither woman had ever heard.

The younger woman's face relaxed, and she

released a sigh of relief.

"Yes, I must."

The Mother Superior moved protectively between the man and the acolyte. She tried to hide her sense of intimidation as she stood before the tallest man she'd ever seen.

"What is this?" the elder nun demanded.

The younger woman put her hand on the Mother's arm. "Magic, Sister, and I must go."

"Are you certain?"

"For once in my life, I have absolutely no doubt."

Reluctantly, the Mother Superior stepped aside and the young woman fell in step with the hooded figure as they walked away. As they left, the older nun was certain she heard purring.

❧❧❧❧

Meekian dozed, as he did so often these days. The grand red dragon, oldest among an ancient race, found that time had become tedious. He lay in his favorite spot in the sun on the stoop outside the entrance to his weyr.

Perhaps I should return to one of the community weyrs, live among dragonkind again. For centuries he had lived this solitary existence deep in the mountains, visited only occasionally by dragons, and even other magical races including unicorns and giants, who sought the wisdom of the wisest of the wise. As he always did when the loneliness demanded his thoughts, he rose and made his way through the cave, breathing fire on torches along the way to light his path. Deep in the bowels of the earth, he looked up at a cavern that held the most precious treasure any dragon could hope to protect. He would not, could not, leave this cave unprotected. Solitude was his to bear for as long as the need demanded. He had willingly accepted that burden when the great dragon mother had called to him, her physical life drawing to an end.

"They're still here, I see," a voice said.

Most would have been startled, but Meekian had lost the ability to be surprised millennia ago. Besides, he recognized the voice.

You are flesh now? he asked telepathically as he turned to face the man with whom he still shared the deepest bond: his rider.

"Yes, it was granted to me," he answered. The man raised a gloved hand, holding it before his face. "The need is near. I will need these hands." He pulled a sword from the scabbard at his side. It shone with the bluish light of magic. "And this sword."

The very one The Lady gave you.

"Yes, the one," the man answered. He replaced the sword to its scabbard, then straightened the simple ringlet crown he wore.

And this is the life you chose to return to as flesh, not as my rider of old? They had been the first to learn of the bond that could be between human and dragon.

Arthur reached out with his mind to answer. *We are always bonded, dear one. You know who I am no matter what flesh I wear, but the people may need a symbol, one they recognize and can follow.*

Yes, I know, Meekian answered. *The time is near.*

Chapter Thirteen

War Games

Greg hung on like his life depended on it. Perhaps it did. He grasped at the leather straps which had failed to hold him firmly in the saddle as the wooden contraption he sat upon wove and bucked at the bidding of the felines manning the ropes giving it motion. Somehow he managed to maintain a grip on his sword as he also clung to the leather. When one of the straw orbs—simulations of the enemy he was to face—swooped near his dangling form, Greg even managed a deft swipe, slicing the straw bundle in half and showering himself in flying straw.

"Stop this damn thing!" he bellowed, managing to catch flying straw in his open mouth and then spitting emphatically get rid of the unwanted intrusion.

He heard laughter as the rope handlers stopped their pulling, instead moving to grasp the edges of the wooden beast, striving to stop its movement. Lithe as always, Lala jumped swiftly to the top of the pseudo dragon, pulling Greg by the tunic as she did so until he was once again sitting upright. Greg grumbled as he loosened the straps, freeing himself of the saddle until he could drop to the ground.

"What use is this?" he demanded. "There's no way this"—he motioned toward the contraption—"can actually simulate the movement of a dragon."

"You did well today, Champion," Lala said as she dropped to stand beside him.

"I felt like a buffoon. There's no dignity to training on...on an overgrown, upside-down wheelbarrow." The feline rope handlers laughed, and, as his temper calmed, Greg laughed with them.

"You are right, my friend," Lala answered, the hint of a purr to the "r" as she said "friend." "That is why you train also on our precious friends, the big cats who are our bearers."

She motioned toward a pride of great cats, each one five to ten times the size of any Greg knew from his world. Lying curled in the sunlight were a tiger, two lions, the smaller and playful lynx upon which Greg trained, and, of course the two cheetahs ridden by Lala and Morris, the leaders of the feline cavalry. Although smaller than the great cats, the speed of those cheetahs ensured the two greatest warriors could be where needed when needed.

Greg rubbed at a bruise on his upper thigh where a strap had held him in place but not without injury. He looked questioningly around. "Where's Morris? He's never missed my training before."

"He has gone to fetch a new recruit," Lala answered.

"Who?" Greg asked.

"Me," a voice answered. They all turned to see Morris, accompanied by a woman, walking between the stone gateposts of the training ground.

Greg stared, puzzled by the sight of a nun wearing the white veil of a novitiate. As they drew near, he struggled to remember who she was, wearing a face familiar yet different. His eyes widened as revelation came.

"Celia?" he asked, taking a step back and placing a hand instinctively on the hilt of his sword.

There was a flash of fear and shame in her eyes as the woman noted his movements. "Yes, Greg, but I am not the woman you once knew."

"God, I hope not," he said.

Celia blushed. "I deserved that."

"This is our training ground," Morris said, a hint of a growl to his voice. "Old battles are put aside here." He placed a hand on each hip and faced Greg squarely. "I was sent by wiser heads than ours to fetch her, Greg the Champion. Do you dispute their commands?"

Greg eyed Celia warily. "You don't know what she did, Morris."

"Yes, we do," Lala said. "All know of her betrayal of the Prophet."

Greg looked at his teachers, beings he had grown to respect and revere. "And you trust her?"

Morris gently grasped the sleeve of Celia's habit. "Do these clothes mean anything to you?"

Greg looked closely at Celia. "They are the clothes of a woman who strives to find God."

"And forgiveness," Celia added, staring at Greg with the glisten of tears in her eyes.

After some moments of silence, the tenseness in Greg's shoulders eased. "No, I don't dispute the commands of the spirits," he said. He looked directly at Celia. "But don't forget, trust lost takes a long time to regain."

"I won't forget," she said.

The sight of two huge shadows halted conversation and drew all eyes to the sky above. A murmur of surprise rolled through the group as two dragons soared from high above, circling to lose altitude and then landing directly before the feline leaders and the two humans. Greg laughed as he recognized the younger of the two dragons.

"Allana," Greg called, pleased at the sight of Kidwell's dragon niece. He knew her from when the young dragon had visited the human world. "What are you doing here?"

The young dragon barely contained her excitement. But she said nothing, instead deferring to the older dragon at her side.

"She is a volunteer," the great red dragon said. "She is here to help train you both to ride and fight."

Greg turned his attention to the red dragon and, for the first time, noted the rider upon him. Perhaps it was the ancient style of gear he wore and weapons he wielded, but Greg forgot the practices of the modern world and instinctively dropped to one knee, his head bowed.

"Greetings, Greg the Champion," Arthur said as he dropped gracefully from Meekian's saddle and walked toward the kneeling man. "Since you have chosen to kneel before me, perhaps it is time to grant you a title befitting your duties." The king pulled his magical sword from its scabbard and tapped Greg lightly on each shoulder. "I proclaim you Sir Greg, Protector and Champion of the Prophets. Rise, Sir Greg."

Greg stood and faced the king. "How are you here? I thought you were dead."

"I am," he answered. "But strange times call for strange miracles."

"Welcome, Meekian," Morris said. "But I do not know your companion."

Smoke puffed from Meekian's nostrils. *We shall*

leave Greg to tell you tales of my rider's many deeds during one particularly eventful life, the ancient dragon thought to his companions.

Lala stepped to face Celia. "If we are to train you, first you must have proper clothing and weapons. Follow me." She turned and strode toward the cluster of buildings that served as barracks and armory. Celia trotted obediently after her.

❧❧❧❧

Aisha felt a sense of completion uncommon for her last brushstroke on a painting. Always—or almost always—she would step back, studying every inch, every dollop of paint, seeing that spot, a focus of final inspiration that would be the coup de grâce to make her work complete. She'd awoken in the early hours, the vision of yet another full-blown painting in her mind's eye. It had been a restless night, sleep troubled by the cold of a bed empty of the man who warmed her and completed her life. Greg had disappeared into the painting of the feline land nearly three weeks earlier, confessing that he did not know when he would return as he left for what he knew would be intense training. Despite weariness, Aisha felt relief at the coming of the vision, something to focus her attention and time as she dealt with an unexpected level of loneliness.

Hours passed. With Greg gone she had to listen to the messages of her body, remembering to eat and drink as she obsessed over the image forming on the canvas before her. She sorely missed his warm meals and kind attention as cheese, crackers, power bars, and caffeine via coffee then soda sustained her through the day.

It was done, totally done. She knew it as soon as the last dollop of yellow ochre completed the wood around the frame of a massive, medieval-style door surrounded by equally massive stone walls. She stepped back to admire her work, then realized it was no longer a painting. Next heartbeat she heard the birdsong above her and felt a warm breeze against her cheek. She looked around. Her home was gone, her paints and brushes vanished, and she stood just outside a tower standing solitary on a green moor. Rolling hills and hardwood forests surrounded a meadow with a brook singing and dancing across the pasture.

"You're just on time," a deep and melodic physical voice said from the ramparts above. Aisha looked up to see a red dragon, scales shining like rubies in the sunlight, leaning over a battlement to look down at her.

Her head tilted questioningly as she admired the creature.

"And you would be Meekian?"

"That I would," he answered, then floated gracefully down to sit curled like a cat beside her.

I met your husband earlier today. His training goes well. Aisha heard his words in her mind as he switched easily to his dragon telepathy.

"Not injured in that training, I hope."

The dragon's chuckle had a deep, musical quality to it. *Perhaps a bruise or two, and I believe a recent encounter with a dragon-riding simulation may have dented his pride.*

It was Aisha's turn to laugh. "That is a wound I can easily help heal once he knows how badly he is missed."

He knows, the dragon responded. *And he*

reciprocates.

The massive door swung open, and Aisha felt a surprise she could not totally contain as the dragon abruptly halved its size, keeping total proportion.

The dragon chuckled again. *How else am I to fit through the door?*

Aisha wiped at a paint smear across the back of her hand and looked down at the disheveled T-shirt and sweatpants she wore. "My apologies for my attire. I did not expect to be meeting a dragon dignitary."

Meekian laughed, even more musical than his chuckle. *Dignitary? I am honored that you think me such, and now there are more "dignitaries" for you to meet.*

"I hope they will not find me disrespectfully casual."

Don't worry, child. These dignitaries see the soul beyond the body.

At his words, Aisha didn't know if she felt fear or excitement. "Who are these 'dignitaries?'"

Some you already know and love, and they all already love you. Meekian looked closely at Aisha. *Perhaps you would prefer if I led the way.*

"Would you please?"

Meekian passed through the doorway into a large chamber, which was surprisingly cheerful considering the cold stone. Bright fires burned in huge fireplaces on each side of the room, and brightly colored tapestries hung on the walls, holding in the warmth of the fires and negating the cold of the stone.

"Ah, Meekian! You've brought her," a man called from his place at a huge table, well laden with meats, fruits, roasted vegetables, and breads, not to mention flagons of drink, pitchers at hand to refill.

Aisha recognized him immediately, not from the legends of her own people but from her husband's obsession with one of the most profound and broadly known legends of the Western World. Not knowing what to do, Aisha bowed awkwardly, contemplating if she should drop to a knee.

"No, no, child." Arthur laughed. "Those times are past." He stepped around the banquet table (not round at all) to stand at her side, a hand gently placed on her shoulder. "Perhaps it is I who should bow to you."

Aisha blushed. "How so?"

"My dear, you are one of the Prophets, the ones whom we have awaited for Millennia."

Aisha shook her head. "I am an artist, nothing more."

"An artist who wields great magic."

Aisha opened her mouth to protest once again, when the musical lilt of Meekian's laughter reverberated in both mind and ear throughout the great hall.

The Great Powers chose wisely in both you and Kidwell. A Prophet needs humility. Otherwise the power would be too great.

The king laughed. "Come, Aisha. We have saved you a place at the table." He gestured to his right, at another long table. Aisha gasped in pleasure as she saw Kadijah and Mohammad smiling at her, an empty chair between them.

Silence had ensued with Meekian and Aisha's arrival, but the cacophony of a feast returned as they made their way to their seats. Aisha received a warm hug from Kadijah as she took her seat, and Meekian ambled to another seat, a stone shelf where a haunch of roasted venison and a platter of roasted vegetables awaited him in a trough ten times the size of the humanoid plates. Humanoid was the word; not all of the bipeds sitting at the table were human. Aisha recognized and waved at Morris. She mouthed the words "How is Greg?" and the feline gave her a universally recognized thumbs-up. As Aisha looked around the U-shaped table configuration, she was not surprised to see a group of three stereotypically gray aliens, but she was rather taken aback at the sight of two tall and magnificent reptilians, resplendent in color with a mix of blues, greens, yellows, and reds mottled throughout their scales. Only one of the two had a plate before her—or was it him? It picked up a chunk of meat and swallowed without chewing. The other simply sat quietly at his place.

"Isn't that reptilian hungry?" Aisha whispered to Kadijah.

"He's already eaten this week," the Prophet's wife responded.

Aisha looked closely at those seated at the head table. All were basically humanoid in form, but with amazing variations. One woman was covered in brilliant blue feathers, and with amazing grace she raised her bowl of food to her face and pecked at its contents with lips that ended in an undeniable beak. The reptilians sat there, next to another that she could only describe as an elf, and she smiled and waved shyly as she recognized Nathanial, the very angel who had sat at her kitchen table enjoying his first experience with the sensation of sour. He smiled in return and raised the pickle wedge from his plate in a private salute. Aisha puzzled at the man sitting at the king's left, especially when she realized that he, not the king, occupied the very center seat of the head table. He had soft brown eyes and waves of dark brown hair with a beard to match. Aisha gasped when recognition finally hit.

"Oh, my God!" she said.

Kadijah chuckled as she followed Aisha's gaze. "Some think so, but he won't confirm our suspicions."

"They think what?" Aisha asked.

"That he's God," Mohammad answered.

"He used to simply nod and smile when asked," Kadijah said.

"Now," Mohammad continued. "He's adopted one of the modern phrases."

"He will neither confirm nor deny," Kadijah added.

Aisha looked back at the gentle man who ate quietly, chatting amicably with the king and others at the table. She took a deep breath, shook her head, and returned to her meal. As she ate, she wondered if she would ever become accustomed to the world of miracles.

At the far end of the hall, beside the platform where Meekian enjoyed his meal, there were two unicorns. One was a beautiful paint and the other a palomino. They shared the same trough and feasted on fresh green alfalfa, so sweet that Aisha could smell its goodness from across the room. Her own plate was filled with delicate and perfectly proportioned slices of turkey, roast potato, a salad of olives and tomato, warm black bread with fresh butter in a dish on the table, and a side dish of sliced cheese and apples.

This food is, well, heavenly, Aisha thought. Then she looked around the banquet hall, wondering where she truly was.

Conversation was raucous and entertaining during the feast. Mohammad told Aisha stories of his childhood, some of which she did not think she would dare share when she returned to her world. Morris, seated near Aisha, leaned forward to see her and gave his purrish account of Greg's encounter with the wooden dragon that morning. His tale left all nearby with tears of laughter in their eyes. Conversation waned as servants magically appeared to remove platters and plates, replacing each one with servings of delicate sweets before each guest. Meekian was provided a whole carrot cake, and the unicorns neighed in delight at the sweet apples placed before them. Glasses of sweet wine and demitasse cups of coffee replaced the goblets of hearty red wine, and the rumble of conversation lowered to a slight murmur as all focused on the delicacies. When almost all had finished the dessert course, the King tapped a knife against a goblet and every murmur evaporated into silence.

"I really have no authority over this gathering," the king said. "But someone had to start the discussion. The Powers that Be asked that I fill that role. Being dead, you see, they figured I was technically an elder to you all." He stood and gestured to his dragon companion across the hall. "With the exception of you, Meekian."

Meekian simply lowered his head humbly. *You were always my voice when needed, dear rider,* he thought, a message intended solely for his rider's mind.

"Right, then. Let's get down to business," the king said. "I assume you all know why we're here."

Aisha looked around shyly, then hesitantly raised her hand.

"Yes, Aisha?" the king asked.

"I have not a clue," Aisha answered.

All present laughed, even Kadijah. Surprised at

the sound, Aisha focused on the musical quality of the reptilian humor. She wondered if that would be the first and last time she would enjoy that sound.

"My dear woman, you play such a critical role it is sometimes easy to forget that we have tasked you with a great burden and rare opportunity to learn the details of the game going on around you," the king responded.

"May I?" Meekian asked, using the slightly harsh physical voice of a dragon.

"Of course," the king responded.

Meekian stood and walked gracefully, despite his size and age, to the center of the hall. "Kidwell has told you of her memories of the great battle over ten millennia past?" he asked Aisha.

"Yes," Aisha answered. "When you all tried to close the portal that enabled demons to enter this universe. It failed, so the veils between the worlds were hardened, and magic was made to deny the demons physical form so that their only power was in influencing humanity."

"That is all true, child, but what you may not realize is that the war has never ended. It has continued for ten thousand years."

Aisha focused on a crumb on the table. She pushed at it with her forefinger. "At some level, I think all humans know that to be true."

"What you may not realize is that very soon we must face the enemy again, as we once did so long ago," Meekian said. *And you, Greg, Kidwell, Maolan, perhaps even Annalome, must play a role*, he thought to Aisha alone.

Aisha gave a sharp intake of breath. It was not news she wished to hear.

As with any war, battle plans are best heard only within the walls of the war room until the life of reality is breathed into them. This hall of generals, heroes, wizards, and healers was no exception. Suffice it to say that the talk went well into the night, requiring an occasional break for participants to stretch their legs or wings and care for whatever bodily functions were required by their species. A second meal of cold meats, bread, and fruit carried them forward, only water and tea to drink so as not to muddle their minds. Aisha heard with relief that she was to be a leader of the healers and prayer warriors but heard with fear that Greg and Kidwell—as Harrana, in her dragon form— would be among the champions on the front lines.

Finally, the council wandered to a close, with agreement achieved on basic plans. After long discussions, the king called for wine and a final toast, a pledge and prayer for the best outcome. As servants distributed goblets and poured the wine, the king looked toward Aisha.

"You look to have a question, child."

"Of a sort," she answered. "It is my artist's mind."

The whole room went quiet, listening.

"Yes?" the king asked.

"Just as white is the light of all color, black is the dark of all color," Aisha said.

"What do you mean?" Morris asked.

"The demons...they have been here for ten thousand years, have they not?"

"Yes," the king answered.

"That is a long time to be among humans. Is it not possible that, even if they are not of the light, at least some may be able to see the colors?" Aisha said.

There was a hiss, although not the unpleasant

sound one may expect, from one of the reptilians. "Yessssss," he said. "Such unexxxxpected thingssss sometimessss matter mosssst,"

The king looked long and hard at Aisha. "We shall see, young one. We shall see."

From across the room, Meekian sat silent, the smile on his face so subtle that only another dragon might recognize it. *Yes, the Powers that Be chose wisely these Prophets. Wisely, indeed.*

The room grew abruptly silent when, for the first time, the man seated at the center of the head table raised his hand, drawing the attention of all present. He spoke softly, yet everyone heard clearly. He had contributed little to the planning of war, although Aisha had noticed tears in his eyes during the making of battle plans, especially during the discussion of possible, even probable, loses on both sides.

"Aisha is right," he said. "Let us not forgot that sometimes the fastest way to defeat an enemy is to help that enemy."

Chapter Fourteen

The Enemy

Pug moved as quietly as he could, which was amazingly quiet considering his millennia of experience as a spy. He sniffed the air cautiously, stepping into a darkened alcove when he detected the scent of approaching soldiers. The spy did not like it there, in the central hallway and caverns so near the headquarters of the Governor. Over the centuries, those demons responsible for watching and reporting had gradually moved to the outlying caverns, those as near the surface as possible for them to still maintain physical form. Besides, they were rarely there, constantly in ethereal form, spying on the lives of humanity. It was lighter there in those outer chambers, the magic of the glowing stones that illuminated their subterranean world had a different hue, even a different taste, nearer the surface. There was a white to the glow, unlike the reds and oranges of the deeper caverns. Pug often thought that they hid in the shadows when spying on humans, and they hid in the light living among fellow demons. Not for the first time, he wondered who he was.

Holding his breath, Pug watched from the alcove as a massive centurion, wearing the stiff, rhinoceros horn helmet of his station, passed, closely flanked by two spear-bearer, each one just a few inches shorter than their massive commander. As they passed, Pug clutched an ornate wooden box to his breast, the purpose for his mission into the depths of the Governor's realm. When he could no longer hear the click of their claws on the stone floor nor, perhaps more importantly, smell the freshness of their passage, Pug stepped once again into the light and walked a route he had not taken for many a turn. As the humans' modern technology improved with electric lights and ever-present security cameras, it was increasingly difficult for him to succeed at the one task that truly gave him pleasure: the retrieval of beautiful things. It was a part of his job from almost the beginning, one that gave him his greatest sense of purpose.

He was relieved when the passage diverged, and he took the lesser of the two tunnels. He approached a guard and drew himself to the fullness of his height, but he was small as all spies tended to be.

"Who be ye?" the guard demanded.

"You know me. I'm Pug the spy."

"So?" the guard said. "Whatcha doing here away from all the horrid light up higher?"

"Ye forgot your job, have you?" Pug challenged. "Don't recall I'm the gift bringer for the Governess?"

"Aye, I recall." The guard spat, and Pug noted the slimy stain on the wall near the guard's station. Looked like he spat often. "But I ain't seen you many a year."

"Damn humans. Can't sneak the stuff like I used to, but I nabbed a good 'un yesterday." He held the box before him, making to open the lid.

"Ah, leave it shut," the guard said. "She likes them pretties, but they don't look pretty to me. She's inside, expecting you she is, although I don't know how."

"Right, then." Pug did not respond to the guard's hinted questions. For as long as he could remember, the Governess had always felt his pending arrival. He placed the box under his left arm, leaving his right hand free to grasp the massive iron ring in the center of a huge wooden door. He turned the handle and the hinges creaked as he opened it, shutting it behind him as he stepped inside.

He took a deep breath and smiled, enjoying the white light of electricity within.

"And what have you brought me today?" a voice asked from across the room.

Pug took time to look around. He loved this chamber, and he had missed his visits. The paintings, sculptures, furniture, and tapestries gave him a sense of pride, since he'd been the one to nab almost all of them.

"Something I know you'll love. The humans call it nostalgia but seems like yesterday to me."

Pug opened the box and held it for the Governess to see. It was a beautiful silver comb and brush set, held in a carved wooden box stained a beautiful mahogany. Although old in design, the materials were new. The Governess picked up the comb and gently tested the strength of the teeth with a clawed finger. It held, and she smiled.

"You remembered," she said. "Ah, my dear Pug. You always remember."

"I know you grieved when ivory teeth aged and broke in the set I nabbed from that French queen."

"The one who lost her head?"

"Yeah, that one."

"My husband laughed in glee when you gave him

that news."

"But the light in your eyes at the sight of the pretties I brought gave me more joy than the Governor's pleasure. Not that I'd tell him."

"Wise imp you are," she responded.

Pug pointed at the comb in the Governess's hand. "Made to look like ivory, but plastic teeth now. Should last a century or two at least." He cleared his throat, embarrassed. "I'm sorry that, well, these pieces can't give you the pleasure they once did," he said. He fought to hide the softness of his heart from showing on his face as he remembered how she had been before evil consumed her, robbing her of her humanity and changing her physically, including the loss of her beautiful black hair.

The Governess looked at him long and hard. He could see a decision fighting to be made in her mind and heart. Slowly she reached for the turban of golden cloth—one he'd nabbed from the markets of Baghdad—and began to unwind it from her head. Tresses of raven-black hair fell to her shoulders, and she lifted the soft bristled brush from the box and began to pull it gently through her soft hair.

He gasped. "Damnation!" He leaned close, looking intently at the Governess's face. Tentatively, he reached a finger to her cheek and rubbed away a streak of the gray-green tint of her face. *Makeup.*

The Governess smiled and waved her hand before her face. Her fanged teeth transformed into perfectly rowed and white human teeth. "He taught me the magic well. Magic I can use now."

"Does he know?"

"That my humanity is returning?"

"Yeah, that."

"Would I be alive and sitting here if he did?"

"You can't let him know."

She laughed harshly. "After all these centuries, do you think me a fool?"

"Never, my lady. Never, but I fear for you."

"And I for you, dear Pug." Her voice changed as she dropped the pretended harshness. She looked around the chamber. "He promised me pretty things." She smiled at the spy. "But it was you who kept that promise."

"As best I could, my lady. As best I could." He allowed himself a smile. "A lovely princess you were."

"But never a queen, and I wanted more," she said. "He kept that promise, to share a grand rule." She bowed her head, staring at her hands as she played absently with the brush. "I never imagined the price."

"I've been honored to serve you, my lady," Pug said.

"And knowing you're there has been a comfort to me."

Embarrassed, Pug shuffled his callused bare feet on the stone. "Begging your pardon, my lady, but I need to go back to the spies' caverns."

"Yes, Pug. I know. The guard will report to my husband if you stay too long." As he turned to leave, she began pulling up her hair and re-wrapping the golden turban. She waved her hand and her fanged teeth returned. "Pug," she called.

He paused and turned. "Yes, my lady."

"You spies, you know much of humanity. You have watched for so long. Do you hate them?"

Pug shuffled and sighed, wondering how to answer. Wondering how much he dared risk. "We watch for their bad, and we report to the Governor, relieved, when we have news to make him happy."

"But?"

Pug gazed directly into her eyes, something he never dared before. "We watch for the bad," he said. "But we see the good, too."

The hinges creaked again as he opened the door and began the long walk back to the spies' caverns.

Chapter Fifteen

Unicorn Flakes

Tommy poured generic frosted flakes in the Superman bowl his mom had left for him on the dining room table. Temporarily banished from the kitchen while his mom baked and dithered, preparing for a dinner party with her boss, Tommy enjoyed his solitude in the dining room. He sat in his usual company dinner place despite the absence of any company or any dinner and smiled as he remembered the painting behind him. He and his mom had wandered into a gallery when they were on vacation in New Mexico, and they'd both stood spellbound before the painting of a unicorn. It didn't look like the other unicorn art Tommy had seen. It was more real than fantastic, and he had never longed to own something more in his life. His mom seemed just as obsessed, unmoving and staring for so long that Tommy had begun to worry.

"Mom?" he had asked. "You okay?"

The woman shook her head, a dazed look on her face. "Yeah, sure, Tommy boy. Isn't it beautiful?"

"Yeah," he answered. He took a deep breath, and whispered, "I want it."

His mom looked around, sheepish. "Me too," she answered.

She stepped to the painting and looked at the small card placed on the wall beside it.

"Acrylic on canvas. Aisha Sudda, Artist," the card read. Tommy's mom gasped when she read the price.

"I see you are moved by Aisha's work," a voice said.

Mother and son startled, unaware anyone was nearby.

Tommy's mom laughed nervously. "Totally smitten," she said, then gestured toward the card. "But it's way out of our price range."

The speaker was an older woman with perfectly quaffed gray hair and wearing a linen suit that probably cost more than the younger woman's entire wardrobe. She touched the frame of the unicorn painting lovingly.

"Aisha's work is, well, magical," the woman said.

"You bet." Tommy looked at the painting longingly. "I want to ride that unicorn." For an instant, he thought he saw the unicorn turn its head to look at him. Tommy rubbed at his eyes with the heels of his hands. When he opened his eyes again, the unicorn was as it had been.

The older woman looked sharply at Tommy but spoke to his mother. "Aisha gave us special instructions for her paintings," she said. "Sometimes, the painting chooses the owners rather than the owners choosing the painting. What can you afford, my dear?"

Tommy's mom laughed, then glanced at her son. "Well, your dad did say I could get anything I wanted for the same price when he got that big-screen TV for his football games." She blushed, embarrassed, then named a price a quarter of that listed on the card.

"Domingo," the woman called toward the rear of the gallery. A ruggedly handsome young man rose from a desk at the rear of the room.

"Yes, Mrs. Springer?"

"We have a sale here. Would you please package Aisha's *Unicorn and Blue Sky* for the new owners?" She turned to Tommy's mom. "Do you need us to ship it to you, or do you wish to take it with you?"

"Uhh…" Tommy's mom seemed too stunned to answer.

Tommy was so excited he was almost dancing from foot to foot. "Will it cost lots to ship it?" he asked. "Dad will be mad if we pack anything more in the Subaru."

The woman smiled at the boy and placed a gentle hand on his head, like a blessing. "I'll cover the shipping."

Tommy's mom recovered from her shock. "That is very generous."

Like they were sisters, the older woman put her arm around the crook of the young woman's elbow and gently guided her toward the desk. Domingo smiled broadly at Tommy and ruffled his hair before carefully removing the painting from the wall.

"You see, my dear," the older woman said. "I, too, was smitten by an Aisha painting. I cannot imagine denying you something that obviously should be yours."

Tommy forgot about his cereal as he remembered that day. Hunger brought him back to the present, and he downed a glass of orange juice then focused on his cereal. Before pouring milk into the bowl, Tommy raised the dish and looked at the now fading comic book image on the side.

Do you think she'll ever realize I'm too old for a kid's dish?

"Does that taste as good as it smells?" a voice

asked right behind him. Tommy felt warm breath on his neck.

His hand froze midair as he reached for the milk, and he turned slowly to come face-to-face with a living, breathing, *speaking* unicorn. The unicorn took a slight step forward so that his muzzle hung over Tommy's shoulder, and he motioned with a dexterous lip toward the bowl.

"This grain stuff, does it taste as good as it smells?" the unicorn asked.

Joy replaced shock as Tommy fully realized his proximity to a unicorn. He took the bowl in both hands and held it toward the animal.

"Try it. You'll like it."

༄ ༄ ༄ ༄

Hank watched the game with dwindling interest. His Lions were losing with little hope of saving the day, but he'd watch it to the end, hoping for more chances to cheer and fewer opportunities to groan. Two beer cans sat on the coffee table, one open and one closed, both in coozies holding the chill. He figured it would be a two-beer game at least, and he didn't want to risk missing an important play for a trip to the fridge.

The house was small, with basic comforts but little to make it special or more beautiful. Since leaving the Army, Hank hadn't had much urge to seek the beautiful. Too many nights were crowded with dreams of the ugly, of what he'd seen, what he'd done in Afghanistan. He went to work, he came home, and watched football on weekends and Monday nights. There wasn't much else for him. He'd dreamed of being a hero, a protector, but he didn't feel like much of either.

There was one thing, though, one item of beauty: a gift from his old commanding officer. It had come UPS with a simple note.

"When I saw this painting, I knew it had to be yours. Hope the Lions kick ass this year," the note said.

The painting was magnificent. Hank hadn't even noticed who the artist was, although he remembered the name signed in the lower-right corner started with an "A." Didn't matter to him, but the painting did. As soon as he pulled it out of the box and yanked away the brown paper, he found himself looking into the most magnificent and regal eyes he'd ever imagined. It was a lion, but not a normal lion. He finished unwrapping the painting and admired the full mane and lion's face atop the body of a nobleman, even a king perhaps. His tunic was blazoned with a golden lion, a sword at his side, and he stood with one foot resting on a rock, a meadow with scattered oaks behind him and a castle in the distance.

He called the CO to thank him, but they spoke lightly, Hank never saying how much the painting moved him yet knowing that the other man understood. The veteran hung the painting on the most prominent wall in his tiny house. It was in the hallway, near the entrance and across from the archway leading to the living room with the couch on just the other side. Almost every morning after he poured his coffee, he spent several minutes standing before the painting, looking at the Lion and feeling like he communed with a friend.

"You understand, don't you buddy?" he asked one day. "That fighting don't matter unless there's something worth fighting for."

For the moment, Hank wasn't thinking about the painting. He wasn't thinking about much of anything except the drone of the sports announcers and the taste of the beer he sipped.

"Looks like they'll lose this one," a voice said.

Hank turned, and there stood the Lion, flesh and blood, not paint and canvas. He jumped to his feet, crouching in a fighting position.

"Careful, or you'll spill your beer," the Lion said. He walked around the edge of the couch. "May I sit?"

Hank stared, mouth gaping. "How the Hell?"

"I have nothing to do with Hell," the Lion said. "Although I have sent a few deserving souls that direction. I'll take your silence as a yes." The Lion sat and motioned with a hand sporting human fingers that ended in lion-like claws. "Is that an extra beer?" he asked.

"Yeah," Hank answered, hesitantly taking his own seat. He popped the top on the second beer and held it toward the Lion.

The Lion drank, and his face grew contemplative as he savored the flavor. "Something like our ales, but lighter. I think I like it."

"How did you get here? Who are you?"

"Forgive me, I must introduce myself." The Lion sat straight. "I am Leopold Manesly the Third, and I came here through that portal." He motioned to the painting. Hank looked that direction and noticed that the landscape remained, but the lion figure was gone. "The gatekeeper has created many portals. This is but one."

Hank reached for the remote, muting the sounds of the game. "Why are you here?"

Leopold took a long drink from his beer before

answering. He set the can back on the table and turned to face Hank.

"I am looking for warriors, but not just any warriors. We need heroes, protectors of the innocent and the good. Interested?"

Hank felt his heart quicken, and he blinked back tears of relief. "You bet," he answered. "Where do I sign up?"

❧❧❧❧

Anna awoke to the sensation of being watched. Despite a full moon shining through the window, it was the deepest, darkest part of the night. She reached for the nightstand and flicked on the lamp there. She blinked in the brightness, but her eyes did not need to fully adjust for her to see the human-sized red dragon seated comfortably on the floor just a few feet from her bed. She gasped, not in fear, but in joy.

"Hello, Meekian," she said. "It is wonderful to see you."

So, you remember? Anna heard the ancient dragon in her mind and heart.

"Yes, I remember." She turned her face away, ashamed. "I remember that I failed you."

I failed you, dear child. I knew your courage, the courage of Harrana, but I did not see that you doubted yourself.

Anna sat up, leaning against the headboard, not worried about this wise dragon seeing her disheveled from sleep and wearing only a long T-shirt. She closed her eyes, remembering.

"I remember the battle clearly. Her voice cracked tearfully. "Too clearly, perhaps, but I only recall bits and piece of that life before I became a rider. I hear again and again, I guess it's my mother's voice: 'Let the men do it, child. Women are weak.' I guess at some level I believed her."

The sound of Meekian's laughter filled Anna's ears as well as her mind. *Women are weak? Ha! But she did not lie, Annalome. She believed what she had been taught.*

"I know," Anna responded. "I fear what you saw in me was false courage."

No, dear Annalome. It took more courage than I can imagine for you to take on an impossible task despite doubting yourself.

"But my doubts doomed us all that day." Tears flowed down Anna's cheeks. "They killed Falong, wounded Kidwell—Harrana—and closed the door between our worlds forever. Those doubts left humanity vulnerable forever."

Forever? But I am here, Annalome. The door is open again. Falong left this side of the veil, but you remember past lives. Surely you know that a soul never ends. And humanity's vulnerability? Child, it was that vulnerability that created the war in the first place. Besides, we now know that the task we gave you was wrong. It could only fail.

"What?"

You don't know how I have longed to tell you that truth, child. Only now, with the door open, is it finally possible.

Anna's tears turned to weeping. "But I was weak when it mattered."

Yes, you doubted yourself. But if you had stood strong, the only outcome would have been your death and the death of your dragon. You would have been carried across the veil as Falong was. Thank all the gods that you were not.

"What do you mean?"

These lives you have lived, you and Kidwell—they have mattered. They matter now, for your task is not done. Do you still doubt yourself?

"Of course. I know there are things no one has the strength to overcome."

That is not what I ask. Do you still doubt yourself?

Anna wiped away her tears and gazed into the dragon's eyes. "If I fail again, it will be because I had not the strength, not because I feared I did not have the strength."

The dragon chuckled. *Those are words that lighten my heart.* He stood, moving slightly toward the Aisha painting hanging near Anna's bed. *We have need of you, Annalome. Be ready.*

Memory overwhelmed Anna, and her tears turned again to sobs. "Will she ever forgive me?"

The dragon paused in his move toward the painting. *Harrana…Kidwell? She already has.*

"No, I know that." Anna wiped at her face with the sleeve of her T-shirt. She took several deep breaths, striving to steady her voice before she continued. "Maolan."

The dragon grew still. Deep pain was visible on his usually inscrutable face. *Then you do remember everything.*

"Yes."

Her anger, hate even, toward you has burned my heart as well.

"Will Maolan ever forgive me?"

The dragon reached to touch Anna's face with amazing gentleness for such a ferocious creature. *I do not know, child. For all our sakes, I hope so.*

Anna watched as the dragon transformed from solid to a red mist and flowed into the painting. She threw back the covers and dressed in her running clothes. There would be no more sleep this night, and she was filled with the desire to run beneath the stars.

Chapter Sixteen

Dreams Like Reality, Reality Like Dreams

A sooty smoke wafted near the ceiling of the stone hallway where Kidwell stood, confused and disoriented. Light flickered from a series of flaming torches disbursed in brackets on the walls. *Where am I?* A massive wooden door creaked open before her, and a demon, short and stocky, stood in the open doorway. Kidwell reached instinctively to where a belt should be, grasping for sword or pistol or whatever she might find there. Instead she grasped only the light cotton of a nightshirt and the elastic band of thin shorts.

"Damn," she muttered, reaching for a torch, the only likely weapon near to hand.

"I won't fight you, miss," the demon said. He looked anxiously up and down the hallway. "Get in here, quick, afore the guard returns."

Kidwell hesitated, her hand on the shaft of the torch.

"I ain't lying," the demon said. "The Mistress, she been wanting to have audience with you, and I always brings her the treasures she wants if I can." There was the creak of another door opening, far down the hallway, and the demon's eyes widened in fear. "Please, inside before we all become roast mutton."

Acting on instinct and faith, Kidwell left the

torch and walked through the open doorway as the demon stepped to the side. She stood, taking in the complexities of a chamber filled with anachronisms—medieval tapestries hung along the walls while a side-by-side refrigerator hummed in one corner. Massive antique furniture was mixed with a lovely Danish modern living room set and a massive four-poster bed had a mattress that looked suspiciously like memory foam. Art from across millennia filled the chamber, ranging from Chinese vases to what could only be a Van Gough painting. Unlike the torches in the hallway, track lighting provided a muted glow.

"Thank you, Pug. You never fail me," a gravelly voice said from a darkened corner of the room. "You can go now."

"But Mistress, she's a quick one. What if—"

"Go, Pug. I'll be safe."

Kidwell turned and watched the stocky demon, more of a gargoyle really, open the massive door and step out into the hallway before pulling it shut behind him. She turned to face the voice, letting her eyes adjust to the darkness.

"Who are you, and why am I here?" Kidwell demanded.

"I am the Governess, consort to the Governor," the voice answered.

"Governor of what?"

The figure stood, stepping into the light. She was much larger than the gargoyle, and Kidwell found her fingers once again reaching for a pistol that wasn't there. The face was distorted and the whole figure covered in scaly gray skin. Despite the beauty of an expensive medieval-style purple robe and a silken dress beneath, there was no beauty to the creature.

"Of Earth, he thinks. The Governor, that is," the figure cackled. She turned sad eyes toward Kidwell. "Of evil, I suppose you'd think. As to the why, you're here so I can warn you."

"Warn me of what?"

The Governess licked her lips, and Kidwell strove to hide her revulsion as she noted the forked tongue. "He's got what he wants, his lackeys rule in key places. Humanity is in grave danger."

"And what would you have me do?"

"Don't know for certain, but sometimes a warning can be enough," the Governess said.

"And what if this is a trap?"

A flicker of hurt crossed the demon's face. "Good question. Looking at me, I don't expect you to think anything else. Take the warning and do with it what you will, but I do have a price."

Kidwell let out a bitter laugh. "Surprise, surprise. What is it?"

"Answer a question."

"You can ask, but I'll betray no one with an answer if it's not a fair question."

To Kidwell's surprise, a tear trickled down the demon's cheek. "When is it too late to change our choices?"

Despite the ugliness, the smell of evil throughout the whole place, Kidwell found herself wishing she felt safe enough to comfort this creature.

"As long as there is will, as long as there is life, we can change our choices," she answered.

More tears slipped silently from the demon's eyes.

"I pray you're right, Prophet. I pray you're right." With no visible transition, Kidwell found herself looking into the face of not a demon but a black-haired beauty with regal blue eyes shining with a profound sadness.

"Who are you?" Kidwell demanded.

The voice changed from gravely to sweet. "I told you who I am," the dark-haired woman said. "Perhaps what you really want to know is who I was."

"Maybe. I don't know."

The woman motioned to a pair of chairs—Danish modern, placed as though she expected a guest. "Sit, please."

Kidwell hesitated. She was in the heart of the home of the enemy. Her mind told her she should flee, but how, to where? Looking at the dark-haired woman, she saw her hostess pouring coffee from a thermal carafe into two china cups. Cream and sugar sat on the same tray as the cups, all placed on an antique side table between the two chairs.

"Cream and sugar?"

"No, thank you, nothing," Kidwell answered, hesitantly taking a seat across from the woman.

The dark-haired woman chuckled as she returned the cup and saucer she'd been holding toward Kidwell to the tray. "You don't wish to suffer Persephone's fate?"

Despite the situation, Kidwell found herself amused. "No, I don't."

"It's only coffee. No pomegranates to be had."

"All the same, I'll play it safe."

The woman's face changed immediately from amused to profoundly sad. "As well you should. Wish I had."

"So, who were you?"

The woman sipped at her coffee, an expression

of pure pleasure on her face. "I don't often have the opportunity to safely return to human form." She waved her hands around her face as if in explanation. "No demon tongue can fully enjoy such pleasure as fine coffee."

"Interesting to know, but back to the question: who were you?"

The woman took a long drink, emptying her cup and setting it reluctantly back on the tray. "I was a princess in a northern land, eldest child of a domineering king. My brother, whom I thought a weak buffoon, was heir to the throne."

"I fear the patriarchy still rules much of humanity," Kidwell said.

"Dear Kidwell, I was wrong. I was the buffoon."

Kidwell sat back, intrigued, forgetting the risks of her situation and eager to hear the rest of the tale.

The dark-haired woman took a deep breath. "I loved to ride alone in the woods, rebellious to my father's insistence that I stay safe on the castle grounds. One day, I met another rider, large, dark, and handsome." The woman closed her eyes and shook her head. "Such a fool I was," she said as she glanced at her listener. "The Governor could appear quite handsome in those days, if he chose."

"Evil can have that appeal, I've heard."

"Almost daily I met this handsome suitor. He sated physical lust, and he offered me what no other had."

"What was that?"

There was a flash of remembered passion in the woman's eyes. "My own throne, the opportunity to rule." She gave a bitter laugh. "He didn't lie, he just didn't tell the whole truth."

"A useful ploy," Kidwell said. "Easiest to hide deep deceit behind a wall of partial truth."

"It took weeks, but he said what I wanted to hear. Only when he saw my lust for power overcame all else did he tell me the price."

"Which was?"

"Far more than pomegranate seeds," the woman said. "It was my brother's blood."

Kidwell made no effort to disguise from her face the disgust she felt. "You killed him?" It was not easily apparent if it was a question or a statement.

"Cut his throat like a pig for slaughter, but he got his revenge."

"How?"

"He woke as the blood gushed from a severed artery." The woman visibly shivered as she continued. "He looked at me not with fear or hate, but only pity and..." She swallowed hard, a hint of insanity in her eyes. "And love. My brother loved me, despite it all."

"Dear God." Kidwell exclaimed.

"God was not there that day. He must have turned his face away in horror." She leaned back, letting the tears flow. Kidwell watched and wondered if that was the first time the tortured woman had released such tears. "I was suddenly elsewhere, in a dark place, wearing a wedding gown that should have been beautiful were it not for the surroundings and the sight of the husband I could not deny, for the Governor now showed me his true form."

"You married him despite that?"

The woman gave a bitter laugh. "Our marriage was sealed the moment my dagger breached my brother's throat. I had not known that he needed me, a human woman, to be his bride. Even demons are bound by some rules. They could not invade the lives of humanity without a complicit partner."

"What a horrible burden to bear, but a choice you could not change," Kidwell said.

Leaning close, the woman grasped at Kidwell's forearm. "Let me say to you what I've longed to say to someone for eternity."

"What?" Kidwell asked, trying to hide her repugnance at the woman's touch.

"That choice," the woman said. A tear escaped one eye and slowly drifted down her cheek. "I would change it. If only I could."

❧❧❧❧

Kidwell awoke with a start and sat straight up in bed. Her nightshirt clung to her by a sheen of sweat.

Maolan moaned slightly, moving in a half-awake state to be closer to Kidwell. "What is it, my *storeen?*" Maolan whispered.

Kidwell lay back in the bed, enjoying the warmth of her lover as they moved in harmony into each other's arms. "Nothing, dear Maolan. Just a dream. Just a dream." Even as she spoke, Kidwell wasn't quite sure that her words were true.

❧❧❧❧

Greg reached for the ceiling in the darkness above him, enjoying the stretch of muscles, sore from recent sword practice. Aisha breathed a steady rhythm in the bed beside him, but he could not sleep. Instead, he looked at his own arms, visible in the moonlight streaming through the bedroom window. He smiled slyly, pleased at the new muscular definition he saw in forearms, biceps, and triceps.

I was born in the wrong time. As much as he loved the study and research of natural sciences, the dominating force of his earlier life, Greg felt a fulfillment in his training with sword, shield, spear, and saddle unlike any he'd ever known before. He did not look forward to battle, to shedding blood, but he did love knowing that he was now a protector for all he loved. Moving gently so as not to disturb his sleeping wife, Greg rolled onto his side, propped his head on one arm, and simply looked at the sleeping Aisha. There was a childlike softness to her sleeping expression that made his heart feel as if it expanded in his chest, needing more room for the love he held there.

"I'll protect you with my life," he whispered, knowing that he meant it from the very depths of his heart.

Greg wondered at his insomnia, something which rarely troubled him. Throughout the evening he'd felt a watchfulness, an electric current at the back of his neck. He recalled a training where Morris had blindfolded him, encouraging him to listen to every sense, to be aware of what he felt but could not see. Moving silently, Morris changed position and Greg was to point toward the feline no matter where he moved. At first Greg failed miserably, but eventually he developed a sense of presence, something not requiring sight or sound. Within only a few days, his pointing finger followed the moving feline without error. When Morris silently motioned for other felines to take place in a circle around Greg, the man dropped his hand, ceasing to point.

"How many are you?"

Morris laughed. "You pass this test, my friend."

Greg pulled off the blindfold and laughed as well. "Guess I got my Spidey Sense," he said.

With a quizzical expression on his face, Morris looked confused and turned to Lala. "Spidey Sense?"

"What is that?" Lala added.

"Uh, it's a fictional character from my world, Spider-Man. He can sense things without seeing them, among other things," Greg responded.

"A spider-man," Lala said. "I have not met one of those." She turned to Morris. "Have you, my husband?"

"No, I have not. Lion folk, unicorns, dragons, reptilians, avian, even ethereal ghosts and energy beings, but never spider people."

"Hey, guys, he's fiction," Greg explained.

"A lie?" Lala exclaimed.

"A made-up story to entertain and inspire," Greg said.

"Oh, a tale," Morris said.

"Yes, a tale," Greg said. "But told through a movie so it looks real."

"Like in the magic boxes of your world?" Lala asked.

"Yes. Exactly like that."

Morris sighed. "I so feel for your people. They live without real magic so must create the illusion of it."

Greg looked at his friend and teacher and felt a sudden and unexpected grief. "Yeah, I guess we have been somewhat deprived."

The man smiled in the dark as he remembered that day. He smiled often thinking of his training, even as he rubbed tincture of arnica on his many bruises.

Then there was a tang, a taste, a smell in the air, and Greg's Spidey Sense jumped to life. He leapt from the bed, drawing his sword—a gift from Morris—from where it leaned against the nightstand.

"Aisha, wake up."

She sat straight up, her eyes wide in surprise and blinking in confusion. "What?"

"Something's wrong."

"What's wrong?" she asked. She rubbed at her eyes with the heels of her hands.

The smell became real, a stench like heated garbage with a side of evil. Aisha covered her nose with her hand.

"Smells like an entire city threw up," she said.

Greg took a fighting stance, his nose raised to the air seeking the source of the stench and moving toward it, not away. There was the danger, and he was the protector. With a pop, a black hole opened in the room and three demons in full physical form leapt through the opening, holding darkened short-swords.

"Run for your studio, for the Morris painting," Greg commanded.

In one fluid motion, Aisha jumped to a standing position on the bed, poised for flight. "Greg, I—"

"Go!" he commanded, moving slightly to create a path between Aisha and the door. All three demons focused on Aisha. Without hesitation, Greg used the distraction. One swift swish of his sword sliced the head of the nearest demon from its body. The other two roared, turning their attention to Greg.

Aisha leapt, covering half the room with one long stride as she lunged for the doorway and then out into the hallway. Greg wished he'd brought his shield as well as sword from the training ground. He grabbed a chair from near the wall. As Greg swung the chair, the clothes resting upon it flew into the air. Greg used that chair to stop one sword thrust while blocking another with his blade. He held up well until the chair proved unequal to the task and shattered into splinters in his hand. As it did so, it diverted the blade of one demon, and Greg successfully sliced upward, opening the beast like slicing a sausage. He blocked the remaining demon's blade with the same swing of his sword, but not before it nicked him in the thigh, adding Greg's blood to the growing carnage in their once peaceful bedroom. Greg took a step back, a hiss of pain his only sign of weakness as he adjusted his stance, moving the uninjured leg to a position of strength.

The twang of a bowstring joined the cacophony of the fight, and Greg felt an arrow pass so close to his side that he sensed the breeze of its passing. He watched in awe as the arrow struck the remaining demon full in the chest, hitting with such force that it pinned him against the bedroom wall, and he hung there, the last flicker of life leaving his face as Greg watched.

Greg turned in a rapid circle, searching for any additional threats. He was relieved to see not a demon but Lala in the bedroom doorway, bow in hand. In the darkness behind, he could see the outline of Morris. As Morris stepped to the side, Greg realized that his friend and trainer stood before Aisha, ready to be the final guard to ensure the Prophet's safety.

Lala stepped into the room, making space for her husband to pass. Morris still grasped Aisha by the arm, keeping her close should there be more threats. He took in the chaos of the room with a quick glance.

"I told you to go," Greg said to Aisha.

"I went to the painting, I called for help, and they

came," Aisha answered.

Morris clapped Greg hard on the shoulder. "You fought well, dear friend."

The wound on Greg's leg ached far more than it should for such a scratch. "Yeah, I guess I did," he responded as his leg buckled beneath him and left him leaning against the bed.

Aisha dropped to her knees beside her husband, examining his wound. "This is dark magic." She walked to the dresser, pulling a small and beautifully designed wooden jar from the drawer."

"It's the balm Kadijah gave you," Greg said.

Aisha pulled the cork topper from the jar. The scent that exuded almost eliminated the stench that filled the room. She dipped her hand inside and spread the smooth mixture on Greg's wound. Visibly and almost immediately it healed, leaving a scar behind.

"You are no longer safe here," Morris said.

"I didn't think they could take physical form," Aisha said.

"Rarely, they can, but only if invited by a human, a human who welcomes the dark magic."

"There's no one like that here," Greg said.

"Perhaps as we open portals to other worlds it is weakening the magic that banished them," Lala said.

"We must inform the elders," Morris said. "Whatever the case, it is time for you both to come with us."

Greg and Aisha hastily jumped into traveling clothes, threw a few important items like the healing jar into a bag, and prepared to leave their precious home. There was a sense of urgency to every move, with Morris and Lala standing ready to fight any new threat. Greg kept his sword held tightly, laying it down only when absolutely necessary to dress or lift an object.

As the four entered Aisha's studio, she gasped with a horrific realization. "We cannot leave my paintings for them to find and use."

Most of her paintings had sold, scattered throughout the world. There were only four or five left in the studio. They worked together, with Lala stepping through the portal to her world and receiving the paintings as the others passed them through. Finally, the three remaining people stepped through the portal to safety. Aisha looked back, seeing her studio from the other side.

"We cannot leave them this access," she said.

Morris looked perplexed. "What do we do?" he asked.

"This is the magic I was given," Aisha said. There was a strength and determination in her voice. "It is mine to protect."

Aisha grasped the sides of the portal. In her hands it took solid form, becoming wood and canvas, converting from a portal to a painting. With all her strength of soul as well as body Aisha pulled, suddenly falling backward, the painting resting atop her fallen form. Concerned, the other three rushed to her side, kneeling beside her, asking if she was injured. She barely glanced at them, instead intently staring at the fallen painting. To their obvious surprise, she erupted into laughter.

"Honey, you okay?" Greg asked.

Still laughing, she pointed at the painting. They all turned to look, astonished to see nothing but a blank canvas.

Chapter Seventeen

It's Time

A double jingle pulled Kidwell from a peaceful sleep. She rubbed at her eyes, her mind striving to recognize the sound when it came again. Maolan sat up in bed, her finger pointing accusingly at the phone on the nightstand.

"It's the invasive magic from your modern world."

Kidwell chuckled as the double jangle came again. She was still unaccustomed to the distinctive ring of a European phone. She rolled over and pulled free the receiver from the old-style, corded phone.

"Kidwell here," she said, at the same time noticing the bright red "3:11" visible on the bedside clock.

"Kid, turn on the news," Admiral O'Hare said, his voice distorted by the distance.

Maolan, still glaring at the phone, turned on the bedside lamp. Kidwell mouthed the words "Admiral O'Hare" toward Maolan. She pulled the pillow up behind her and sat awkwardly against the antique headboard.

"Admiral, it's three a.m. and there's no TV in this cottage."

"You got Internet, don't you?"

"Sure."

"Well go to CNN or ABC or BBC, Hell you can use Fox News if you want, just turn on the damn news."

"Hold on," Kidwell said. She turned to Maolan. "Love, this sounds urgent, please bring me my laptop."

Naked, Maolan threw back the covers and strode with obvious irritation out of the bedroom toward the larger main room, returning almost immediately with the computer in her hand.

"What's going on, Admiral?" Kidwell asked as she waited for the computer to boot up.

"This makes Desert Lightning look like kindergarten," he said.

His words made her heart grow cold. She knew how close they'd come to a world devastating war when magic first made its return to her world. Then she remembered the dream, the Governess's warning. Her mouth went dry and her palms sweat. Maolan crawled back under the covers, watching Kidwell's face intently. Kidwell could feel the cold her naked lover brought back to their bed, and she moved close, taking one hand from the computer and pulling Maolan closer in order to share her body heat.

"You there yet?" the Admiral asked.

"Hold on. Just logged on."

Kidwell hit the bookmark on her browser for a common news site. The newscaster was mid-sentence, but Kidwell didn't hear the words. She simply read a ribbon phrase trailing across the bottom of the screen. "An estimated 15 warheads are aimed at the US. US intelligence reports they are currently in armed-and-ready status."

Maolan looked at the computer then focused on Kidwell. "What does it all mean?"

"Shhhh." Kidwell raised one hand in a gesture of waiting. "Let me listen."

The story was grim. Kidwell had neglected the

world for nearly six months, simply enjoying a peaceful life in Ireland as her love grew for the only woman who could ever ease the ache left by Anna's betrayal. Now she had trouble breathing past the guilt of her neglect. She had no idea how bad it had become in such a short time.

It was a second-level world power, one long known as a "loose cannon" controlled by an irrational and egocentric dictator. The news now reported a horrific scenario, with the US's own current despot starting a row over…over the size of their dicks as near as Kidwell could understand. Reports of a nuclear arsenal now at the dictator's disposal were underestimated, and both countries stood ready to launch. What's more, other world powers, unsure of US stability, were placing their nuclear launch capabilities on standby.

"Jesus help us," Kidwell mumbled.

"I was kinda counting on you, Kid," the Admiral said. "We need a miracle, and you and Aisha are the only ones I know who seem to keep a pocketful of those around."

Kidwell saw vague motion at the foot of the bed and glanced up to see White Buffalo Calf Woman standing there. Maolan jumped from the bed, intimidating despite her nudity as she took a fighting stance.

"It's okay, Maolan. She's a friend." Kidwell smiled at the…well, what was she? A goddess? A spirit guide? *A friend*, Kidwell thought. "Maolan, meet White Buffalo Calf Woman. White Buffalo Calf Woman, meet Maolan."

Maolan relaxed immediately, kneeling as though before royalty. "'Tis an honor."

"Rise, Maolan," the spirit said. "It is time. Dress,

both of you. We must go."

"Gotta go, Admiral," Kidwell said into the phone. "Seems a pocketful of miracles may have just arrived."

め め め め

Kidwell and Maolan stood on a hilltop, White Buffalo Calf Woman beside them. Kidwell was accustomed to magic, to teleportation, to interacting with mystical beings, but this was a rare experience. She stood not in in her astral body but in full physical form. Hesitantly, she reached one hand toward the spirit being beside her and felt warmth as her fingers connected with the legendary figure standing, fully physical, beside her.

"Yes, I am real at all levels here," White Buffalo Calf Woman said. "As are you."

Not only that, but the place felt odd despite a sense of familiarity. Kidwell studied the terrain with low mountains to her right and rolling plains to her left with a dry riverbed running between, but it was different somehow, making it difficult for her memory to place from what time she had known it. Bare desert was all around, but her mind wanted to impose green grass, spreading trees, and flowing water.

"The battle," Maolan said. "It is where we fought the battle?" The warrior pointed across the shallow valley to the desert beyond. "Falong fell there."

Kidwell gasped as she realized the truth of Maolan's words. She turned to face her lover, surprised to see tears in her eyes and flowing down the cheeks of the staunch warrior. She was even more surprised to feel tears in her own eyes, signs of a grief she did not realize was still there. *This is where it all began, where all that was before ended.*

You have come. Kidwell heard the voice in her mind. She turned and felt relief and joy at who she saw.

"Meekian," she called. Together, she and Maolan ran to their master, their teacher, the wisest of all the dragons. Despite their human forms, they stood on each side of the dragon's head, lowered in welcome, and gave the traditional dragon greeting touching forehead to forehead.

I welcome you both, two of the original Four of our vanguard, in any form you wish. But I ask that you now be dragon, for we need you to bear riders this day, Meekian said mind-to-mind to both women.

"But Maolan is the only rider," Kidwell said.

"Oh no, she's not," Greg said, stepping forward.

Kidwell gasped at the sight of him, fully dressed in light armor, a quiver filled with arrows and bow strapped to his back, sword at his side, and a long spear in his hand. To his right stood two magnificent feline warriors, each also armed. Nearby lay two massive cheetahs, twenty times the size of a normal cat, each saddled and wearing light armor as well.

"Greg?" she said, astonished.

"I've been training."

"As have I," said a hesitant voice.

Kidwell turned. A few yards away stood a woman, also armed and armored, her hand resting on the shoulder of Masat, Kidwell's adopted dragon sister who was already saddled and armored for battle as well. A wash of confused emotions filled Kidwell as she recognized the woman.

"Celia," she said coldly, remembering clearly the woman as she had been—naked and gloating over her seduction and conquest of Kidwell's soulmate, Anna.

"Kid, she's changed," Greg said. He stepped beside Kidwell, placing an arm around her shoulders. "We need her, and she needs to make peace with us."

"You know her, Greg?" Kidwell fought a sense of betrayal.

"I knew her then, and I know her now. I swear, it's like two different women; one I wouldn't trust to take the garbage out, and another I'd trust with my life."

Kidwell glanced toward Celia, waging an internal emotional battle. She turned to Greg and looked long and hard into his eyes. "I can't yet trust her, but I can trust your judgement. I'll have to have faith in that."

"*Aghrá*, look around," Maolan said.

Kidwell obeyed. For the first time, she noticed that Meekian was both saddled and armored. Standing at his side was a tall man, salt-and-pepper hair and beard, and an iron circle—a crown—upon his head.

I never told you, Meekian telepathed. *That I was the first to take a rider, but he had passed his first life and begun human incarnation when I first knew you. Please, meet Arthur.*

"Arthur?" She looked at the man in astonishment. "Are you actually—"

"Yes," the man interrupted. "But that was lifetimes ago. I take the form now only because I must lead in battle. Today, I am simply your companion in arms." He raised both arms in a gesture encompassing all around them. "Look around you. See what we both must inspire and lead this day."

Again, Kidwell obeyed. They stood before a massive gathering, organized pockets and groups, grouped as battalions, but each group bore a personality. Nearby, she saw a large contingent of Native Americans, most dressed in traditional attire including war paint. At their very edge she saw a tall young man, one whom she would know at any distance.

"Martin," she called. At her call, both Greg and Maolan followed her gaze. They all waved enthusiastically. "Come over," Kidwell yelled to her young friend. Martin raised his hand, still holding a war lance in the other. They could see the smile of greeting on his face, but he gave a broad gesture that said clearly that he could not leave his people.

Felines had their own camp, encircling a remuda of oversize cats intermingled somewhat with a pride of lions. Beside the lions a ragtag group of humans, wearing bits and pieces of military uniforms, carried rifles with bayonets affixed.

"Our veterans," Kidwell said, a note of pride in her voice. "But their rifles won't work here."

"No," Greg answered. "But their blades will. They've been trained with bayonet and knife. We didn't have time to teach them swordcraft."

From this motley group, a man dressed in full Battle Dress Uniform waved to them, and Kidwell recognized Admiral O'Hare. His wave ended abruptly as two men approached him. His attention changed focus to those men. Kidwell had no doubt he was in command. Unicorns, even reptilians, and a small but important contingent of avians were visible along with a whole array of humanoids, some so alien that Kidwell had no name to give them. She glanced back at her close group of comrades.

"Where's Aisha?" she asked Greg.

Greg looked to Meekian as though seeking permission to speak. "She's part of a...well, secret mission."

You will know her mission soon enough, Harrana, Meekian thought to Kidwell, using her dragon name. *For now, we must organize your mission.*

Kidwell returned her focus to the immediate area. *Four dragons and three riders...*

"We're still short a rider," she said.

"No, we're not," a painfully familiar voice answered. Kidwell turned to the woman who now stepped into view from behind Meekian.

"Anna," she barely choked out, emotion robbing her of her voice.

Maolan stepped forward, her hand on the hilt of her sword. A heartbeat behind her movement, Meekian adjusted so that his face occupied most of Maolan's line of sight.

Would you raise your hand to one of the Four? He questioned the warrior but broadcast his thoughts to all around them.

"But she...she failed us," Maolan said.

I failed us, Meekian answered. *I was naïve in thinking simple magic could master grand evil. If Annalome failed, it was because she was given an impossible task.*

Maolan's stance spoke of uncertainty, something Kidwell had never before seen in the confident fighter. Some moments passed until Maolan finally took a step back, still focused on the wisest of dragons.

"I shall bow to your wisdom," she said.

Meekian also stepped back. A triangle formed. Kidwell, Anna, and Maolan stood close, but with an unspoken wall in the short space between them.

"I cannot ask either of you to forgive me," Anna said. "I ask only that you allow me to stand this day, not to disprove any cowardice in the past but to prove that mistakes of the past need not rule the present."

They wept, all three. Finally, Maolan turned, looking to the ground as she spoke.

"So be it," she said, wiping viciously at her tears with the leather vambrace on her forearm.

Kidwell faced Anna, saying nothing. Anna's eyes alone pleaded for her answer.

Kidwell stepped back, the determination on her face shadowing her tears. There was a flow of light and shadow, then Kidwell was gone, a luminescent black dragon with the sheen of rainbow standing in her place.

My rider again? asked Harrana the dragon.

Your rider again, answered Annalome.

Following suit, Maolan transformed into a magnificent green dragon nearly twice the size of the black dragon beside her. Only those unfamiliar with dragons would fail to recognize that the greater power rested in the smaller dragon.

Greg and the feline Morris stepped forward, each carrying a saddle and components of a dragon's light armor. Dragons wore little armor, for their strength lay in speed and maneuverability. Heavy armor was more a liability than a benefit. Annalome took a saddle from Greg, in doing so taking responsibility for equipping Harrana. As soon as the straps were set for saddle and armor, Annalome leapt to Harrana's back, placing and tightening the straps to hold her in the saddle no matter her dragon's maneuver. Anna accomplished the task with such speed and precision it looked as though it had been hours, not millennia, since she last took that seat. Greg did the same—albeit with less confidence—to secure his saddle on Maolan.

During the flurry of action, Arthur had already taken his place on Meekian. The eldest of dragons looked with obvious pride at the two pair of dragons and riders before him.

We have our Four, our vanguard, again. Fly with us, he directed. *There is more you must know.*

With that, the grand old dragon launched into the air with a roar. Arthur drew his sword, waving it above his head in defiance. The two younger dragons launched and roared on the tail of their leader. With Meekian at the front and Harrana and Maolan as his wingmen, they flew in a broad circle over the entire army. Unbidden, those below cheered the dragons flying above, raising a cacophony of defiance that echoed throughout the mountains, desert, hills, and valley. It was a moment that thousands would remember as one of the most glorious of their lives.

East they flew, with a speed Harrana had rarely dared achieve. She glanced with concern at Maolan, knowing that it required all the strength of the winged dragon to keep pace with those that flew by magic alone. Just as Maolan began to fall ever so slightly behind, before them they saw a dome of glittering blue light and Meekian slowed the pace, leading them to a hillside overlooking the light.

Once safely on the ground, Harrana moved close to Maolan. She touched forehead to forehead with the green dragon, willing her friend and lover her energy. Annalome dropped to the ground and stepped to Maolan's side.

"Are you all right?" The green dragon simply looked at Annalome, but for an instant she leaned closer to the woman, and Annalome dared a brief healing touch to the dragon's shoulder.

Look to the light, Meekian thought to them all.

As Harrana looked, she could see that at the center was a large gathering of beings—mostly human, but not all. She saw a gentle giant among the crowd, and near the center she saw a man, long hair and beard, dressed in a long, coarsely woven robe. He was seated cross-legged, his eyes closed. The same was true of almost all in the group, including Aisha, whom she saw seated near the man. When Greg saw her, he leaned far forward in the saddle. Harrana could almost taste his longing to be near his wife. The entire crowd exuded a hum of sound, some singing, some chanting, some just quietly humming, but all in a harmonious noise.

What is happening? Harrana asked Meekian. Arthur heard and answered.

"They're praying."

The mistake we made, Meekian added. *Was thinking that simple magic could counter great evil. There is only one magic powerful enough to heal that.*

"Love," Annalome said.

They all turned to look at her.

Yes, Meekian answered. *Love, that is our secret weapon.*

Then why must we fight? Harrana asked.

To give them time. And to pray with them for the seed of Love among the demons, for that is the seed that must flower.

"Will it be there?" Greg asked.

For that, we call on another magic: Faith, Meekian answered.

As she looked, Harrana noticed something swirling in the blue light surrounding the devout. She though she caught glimpses of spirits in the light.

The Matrix? she asked. *Is it the Matrix, like when Desert Lighting was defused and the weapons stopped?*

Yes, it is the Matrix. Meekian looked in wonder at the blue light. *Tomorrow many beings of good heart will awake from dreams of great import.*

The dragon version of a cleared throat sounded behind them. Harrana turned to see her niece, grown more mature in the months they had been apart. Harrana rushed to the young dragon, heartily giving the forehead to forehead greeting.

Allana, what are you doing here?

Waiting. I'm to be a messenger between the healers and the battle.

Your brave niece wanted to fight, Meekian added. *But we had a more important job for her. Now, my vanguard, you Four must return to the army. Rest, eat, prepare yourselves. Arthur and I have business here before we can return.*

Harrana gave her niece a farewell, moving beyond the forehead acknowledgment to wrap her long neck over the young dragon's shoulder. A hot tear dripped from her niece's face and hissed on the green grass.

Be safe, Allana said. *Tell my mother to be safe as well.*

I will, Harrana answered.

Annalome was once again in the saddle, and the four of them took to the air. Due West they flew, knowingly going toward harm's way.

Chapter Eighteen

Still Before the Storm

Kidwell looked above. Despite the hours since the angels first arrived, she still stared, astonished at the sight. The angels were of various sizes and mostly dressed in white, although a smattering of red and gold could be glimpsed in robe and aura. Some hovered above, gliding on thermals in lazy patterns like eagles watching the world beneath. A smattering of low clouds had arrived with them, like obedient pets. Kidwell had no idea how many rested within or upon those clouds, but she could see bits and pieces of those on the edge, passing the time as though awaiting a battle involved no fear or stress. Kidwell felt certain one group played cards seated in a circle as though a cloud were as solid and comfortable as any chair. She saw harps and horns and heard those instruments, along with many voices. The music they made filled the background with a harmonious cacophony.

"I wonder if Nathaniel and Angela are among them," Greg said from behind her.

Kidwell startled. She hadn't realized he had followed her as she'd walked from the tension of the camp. Taking human form, Kidwell sought a moment of peace. As human, it was easier to block her empathic connection to the general fear in the air as thousands awaited battle. Even more distressing was the unspoken conflict between Maolan and Annalome. She knew they both sought to stifle the broadcast of their soup of emotions, but Kidwell was too close, and they both mattered to her too much. She wished the air could be cleared, but none of the three dared distract their focus from the battle to come.

"Who are Nathaniel and Angela?" Kidwell asked. Still looking above, Kidwell noticed two angels take flight, leaving the comfort of their cloud.

"The angels who came to our house," Greg said. "I think Aisha told you about them." A broad smile covered his face as the two angels flew directly toward them. "Speak of the"—he laughed—"well, not the devil. Here they come."

Towering over Kidwell—the male had to be at least seven feet tall—the angels landed gently just a few feet from the two humans.

"You called?" the female said.

Greg laughed. "Good to see you both." He turned to Kidwell. "Nathaniel, Angela, I want you to meet Kidwell. Kidwell, this is—"

"Let me guess, Nathaniel and Angela." Despite all the miraculous things she'd seen, beings she met, Kidwell was a tad awestruck to be in the company of angels.

"And we know who you are," Nathaniel said. "Half of the Prophet pair and leader among dragons."

Kidwell blushed. "Sounds way too grand when you put it that way."

The two angels looked directly at each other. Kidwell did not hear the message, but she felt the residual flow of a telepathic thought.

"Greg, my friend, did you happen to bring pickles?" Angela asked.

Greg laughed. "Sorry, don't have any in my field rations."

"Ice cream?" Nathaniel asked.

"Even harder to pack," Greg said. An expression of grief flashed across his face. "If Aisha and I are ever able to return home, you are welcome to visit any time. We'll make sure to keep a supply of pickles and ice cream."

"Pickles and ice cream?" Kidwell couldn't help but feel astonished. Unbidden, her gaze fell on Angela. *Can angels get pregnant?* she wondered.

Greg's raised eyebrows said that he knew exactly what she was thinking. "Um, Angela and Nathaniel had never experienced sour before they visited our house. They loved the pickles, and, along with the felines, they all acquired a taste for ice cream."

"Oh," Kidwell responded. It sounded lame, even to her ears. She gathered her dignity and continued. "I cannot tell you how glad I am to see you all in the skies above."

"We shall protect from above as best we can," Nathaniel answered. Above, one horn blew louder than the rest. The two angels glanced toward the sound. "We must return." He placed a hand on Greg's shoulder. "I shall see you again in happier times, my friend."

"If we survive, that is," Greg responded. He looked surprised as Kidwell and the angels laughed.

"Greg, my soul-brother, think about it," Kidwell said. "They're angels. Live or die, you'll see them again."

A smile brightened his face. "Suddenly, I feel better than I have all day."

The horn blew again, and both angels took flight, waving as they left.

"Wow, Greg. You have friends in high places," Kidwell said.

"Well, you can't have all the luck, you know."

Their conversation ceased as they saw Meekian take to the air, flying directly toward the hilltop where they stood. As he flew, Kidwell took dragon form.

Greg looked at the dragon towering beside him. "It never ceases to amaze me when you do that."

A puff of smoke escaped Harrana's nostrils as she chuckled.

Meekian landed neatly beside the pair. He and Harrana touched foreheads in greeting, then the elder dragon turned to Greg.

My apologies for the interruption. Both dragon and man heard the message in their minds. *But I have need of private conversation with Harrana.*

"No problem," Greg said. He pointed down the hill to where Maolan lay curled, her head raised and her gaze watching the three of them on the hilltop. "I was going to ask Maolan for some more air time anyway. Need to get as comfortable as I can riding her in the time we have." He nodded respectfully to Meekian and saluted jauntily toward Harrana before striding down the hill.

Meekian did not pause to acknowledge Greg's departure, turning immediately to Harrana. *We have much to discuss and not much time.*

We have our battle plans. Is there more? Harrana asked.

Important matters, indeed.

What are they, wise one?

We are the last of our kind, he thought. *It may be that both or neither of us survive this battle, but if it is you alone, you must assume the mantle of leadership.*

I am not ready, Harrana responded.

Meekian's laugh could be heard by both mind and ears. *And now you learn a great secret. Anyone who thinks they are ready for leadership most certainly are the ones who are not ready for that authority.*

I shall pray with all my heart that you will be there to guide us before, during, and after this battle.

Harrana felt a wave of sadness from the elder dragon. *Ah, dear child, I am old even for the eldest of the elder race of dragons. I am tired, and I would have willingly crossed the veil long ago had not the need been great.* He gazed deeply into Harrana's eyes. *The powers above us all have given me this time with my rider, but he does not belong here. I pray for that time when we are together again on the other side of the veil.*

Harrana thought of the depth of the grief she felt when her relationship with Annalome was severed. For a moment she could not breathe, imagining that pain extended over thousands of years.

Then I shall pray instead for the greater good, whatever that means for both of us.

I have much to tell you, the elder continued. *Should I pass, you must go to my solitary cave. There is a reason beyond meditation for my centuries of hermitage. Hidden deep within is a treasure that can only be released once this evil influence is exorcised from our universe. You must become its guardian, and its liberator.*

What is this treasure?

You will see if the need arises. He leaned close. Harrana realized that if they had been speaking, his would now be a whisper. *And this is a secret only those of our race can know, or use. Even deeper in my cave is a reflective pool. There you can seek, see, and hear the guidance of our ancestors, even back to the time when we were simply light, not yet taking a physical form. They will speak to you if they will. They will remain silent if they see that you must find your own answers.*

Harrana looked around her, at the armies surrounding them. She thought of the battle plans so heavily dependent on Meekian's wisdom. The fear of the coming battle now seemed pale compared to the weight of responsibility she may face as Meekian's heir.

Is there no one else, no one better qualified as your successor?

Your question only strengthens my confidence that it must be you.

Harrana looked at her friend and master. The thought of losing him filled her with a deep grief.

If it comes to that, I shall do my best.

That is all I ask. Meekian said nothing more, and he curled at her feet. Surprised, Harrana realized he was sound asleep. She sat beside him, guarding the elder and feeling a profound pride as she realized the depth of his trust in her.

Chapter Nineteen

Armageddon

Harrana looked to the sky as it morphed into a circle of darkness amidst the blue. Ten thousand years didn't matter; she remembered that sight. The portal to a dark world opened—almost. The raven-colored dragon knew untold numbers of demons waited on the other side. She could hear their roars of frustration, unable to pass the magic barrier that kept them at bay. The outcome of the day's battle would determine if they would pass freely or be forever banned. She felt her own tension, and she felt that same cold, consuming fear as her mind joined with her rider, the rider she had known in her human form for many lifetimes. Yet, there was comfort. They faced terror, sought for courage, but not alone. The strength of two together was far greater than the strength of two alone.

Another roar joined the cacophony from the sky above. In the bare desert before them, Harrana now saw the army of earthbound demons, not in the nonphysical form that had been their fate since the last war, but as full-fledged in-the-flesh beings. They were real and so were the blades, axes, and engines of war that came with them—unseen one moment, appearing as legions the next. Meekian and the generals had warned it would be such. In the dimensional barriers of this liminal space, both armies had formed on the desert plains and hills, totally unseen by the other. With the opening of the portal, those barriers were gone. Harrana felt the wave of fear not only in her own heart, but in the hearts of the warriors in the fields around her. The sight was terrifying. There had been no real estimate of the enemy's number, but there seemed an unbroken field of undulating blackness before them, demons in multiple shapes and forms. Near the front of the demon army surrounded by soldiers, a fully armored demon sat upon a wood throne that rested atop a massive wooden wagon, pulled by four demons so large that Harrana suspected they were actually trolls. A smaller throne was to his side, and Harrana could spare only a moment of recognition of the Governess who had summoned her to the demon caves. She spared an even longer thought to the mysterious object on the wagon beside the Governor and covered by a large canvas. A special coldness wrapped itself around both Harrana's and Annalome's hearts as they saw that many of the demons had developed wings since the battle millennia ago. With only four sets of dragons and riders, that was especially daunting. Meekian had allowed a handful of solitary dragons he deemed ready to join the fight, but their fire would not last long. Without sword, lance, and bow at their backs, their effectiveness would be brief and their vulnerability great.

Thank God for the angels, Annalome thought to her dragon.

That is most certainly the right one to thank, Harrana responded.

They both chuckled at the unintended joke, and the laughter evaporated a huge chunk of their fear.

Harrana realized she must fight a battle before the battle, not against demons but against fear. She thought a brief warning to her rider, and Annalome leaned low in the saddle as Harrana rose a few yards in the air, just high enough to be seen by all their comrades in arms in the fields around them. She let out a roar that tore through the air, the loudest and longest she'd ever managed or even attempted. Alone she almost managed to dwarf the cacophony of bellows from the army of demons they faced. Behind her, from the enclave of generals, Harrana heard her roar echoed, and she knew Meekian's voice. Almost in unison with Meekian, huge roars erupted to her right and her left, and Harrana knew Maolan and Masat had added their call to battle. The effect rippled throughout the allies. Voices of many species joined in, and the rattle of spear on shield filled the air, finally silencing the battle cry of the enemy. Harrana and the other dragons drifted back to earth, and the sounds around them faded to a silence so profound Harrana felt they'd entered the eye of the storm. They waited, all of them, for the order to fight.

Harrana knew that Annalome held a key to the battle, not to winning it, but to distracting the enemy from the real strategy. She held an exact replica of the plain, five-foot-long wooden wand she had wielded in the first great battle—the one that had failed to close the portal. True, this one held real magic, but they knew it would fail. More was needed than closing the portal; they knew that, but the enemy did not. Their orders were to draw demons toward them, to feign efforts to reach the portal, and, at the right moment, to give the enemy false hope by failing at their effort. Meekian made it very clear that they were not to risk their lives saving a nearly useless wand, but Harrana knew they would still be the focus of the demon offensive. It was a horrifying thought.

A great horn blew, and Harrana took to the air, Maolan and Masat moving immediately to protect her flanks. She glanced over her shoulder long enough to see Arthur and Meekian take to the air as well, positioned over the great ally army. It was King Arthur who blew the horn, a sound so grand that Harrana did not doubt rumors it had been used at Jericho. As planned, the wing of dragons circled above the ally army with an initial mission of bolstering courage for the mounted and foot soldiers below. As they flew, cavalry moved rapidly to each flank of the vanguard infantry consisting of reptilian warriors, most of them at least eight feet tall and armed with shield, spear, and sword. Behind the reptilians, ranks of archers waited, arrows nocked but bows unbent. The archers worked with surprising uniformity considering the amazing mix of humans, felines, even tall white aliens. Cavalry on the right flank, comprised of felines mounted on their huge cats, also moved with military precision, but the cavalry on the left flank was a hodgepodge of mostly humans—cowboys armed with ropes, bowie knives, and a smattering of old-style cavalry sabers; medieval living historians with freshly sharpened swords and unpainted lances, hewn from the strongest wood and tipped with sharp metal instead of those intended to break away without injuring an opponent; Bedouins riding magnificent Arabians and waving curved scimitars; and there was even a mix of riders of all sorts bearing anything that might suffice as a weapon, the pitchfork being the most common. Harrana noticed with pride and fear that her dear Martin, the son of her soul, rode at the head of a contingent of indigenous peoples, mostly Native American. Even in haste she saw that his Apache face was painted in Cherokee colors, and she knew it was in honor of her and her heritage.

That moment was the last opportunity Harrana had to make sense of the battle below.

Martin's heart felt cold as he looked above. His soul-mothers flew into the greatest danger he had ever witnessed, and he could do nothing but force himself to move his focus from the skies to the wall of demons before them. He led the warriors at his back, and he reminded himself that the most he could do for Kidwell and Anna, for all humanity, was to win the fight before him, as small as that might be in the scheme of the war. He glanced above again, in time to see a contingent of winged demons heading directly for the dragons and riders. He let his lance drop to his lap and the shield to hang from the horn of the saddle. His bow was bent, and an arrow flew, catching the lead demon in the wing of attackers. As though on command, a flight of a hundred arrows followed his own from the archers stationed behind the infantry of reptilians.

A whoop and yip of war cries erupted from those around him, and Martin realized his mistake. He was to command, not depart on personal vendettas, and he held the bow to the side, calling loudly in Apache to stop his eager warriors from leaving their position for a foolish and hopeless charge into the midst of the enemy. He knew the job of the cavalry in the battle plans.

The infantry of reptilians moved as planned, and even Martin was surprised at their numbers as they marched forward, forming multiple ranks at the front of the battle. With great discipline, they formed walls of shields and spears that looked impenetrable to Martin's inexperienced eyes.

Martin heard the old-fashioned bugle from the living historian who now rode beside an actual general of the British Army. This day the call of that bugle did not teach history; instead, it helped make it. In the relative quiet before the battle, this hodgepodge cavalry had been instructed on the bugle calls and flag signals the general would use to direct those under his command. Although there was a marked absence of designated columns and ranks, the left flank cavalry moved neatly to their designated positions. The weight of the land battle rested with the trained and terrifying infantry, but the cavalry bore the responsibility of protecting the flanks, ready to charge should any demon forces move to pose a threat from the sides or even the rear. Martin's company bore a separate responsibility from others in the cavalry, for unlike the others, they could fight from a distance. With firearms useless in this magical liminal space, bows and arrows were critical. The indigenous peoples he commanded formed a second rank as they took position. Martin gave the command, and all others in his contingent hung lances and shields from their saddles and readied their bows. Although not at the front of the cavalry, they were the first line of defense for any threat to the flank.

☙ ☙ ☙ ☙ ☙

For Harrana and her wing of dragons, the focus was in the air. A contingent of nearly twenty winged demons, long spears or bows in hand, dared to fly toward the wing of dragons and riders, making straight for Harrana and Annalome, focused on the staff Annalome held. They were still low in the air and a flight of arrows from the archers below struck half the demons from the air. Harrana saw that the first arrow to fly came not from the ranks of archers, but from the cavalry, and she felt pride as Martin's arrow hit true the wing leader of the demons. As injured demons fell within the midst of the reptilian infantry, the spears of the soldiers finished the job begun by the archers' arrows. The remaining demons rapidly rose in the air, out of the archers' range. Harrana, Meekian, and Masat flew in tight formation, briefly enjoying the relative safety of the air above the archers.

We must fly through them. Harrana heard the thought of her rider.

Of course, she responded, somewhat tersely. She focused on the internal fire she held within, stoked with sulfur stone before the battle and held in bay for when needed. The bane of dragon fire as a weapon was that it lasted for only a few powerful bursts. As wing leader, Harrana lifted her elevation, seeking a path as far from the waiting winged demons yet making for the gaping hole of the portal. As they circled upward preparing to meet the demons flying above, Harrana noticed a dark cloud rapidly rising from the back of the demon army. Her heart went cold as she recognized it for what it was. The relatively small vanguard of winged demons had given her hope. Now, over a hundred flew to meet the tiny wing of three pairs of dragons and riders.

Holy shit, Harrana thought. Her mind heard a cacophony of responses from Annalome, Maolan, Masat, and Meekian, but their messages basically echoed her own. Harrana roared, her mind and heart squared and set for whatever came, and she changed to a direct course toward the portal.

Fly, my love, Annalome said. *Take us to our fate, whatever that may be.*

So, Harrana flew straight to her target until two winged demons obstructed her path. She dodged an arrow loosed by one and directed a burst of flame that decimated the winger archer and singed his companion. She heard Annalome scream in frustration, and she saw the wand, the one to close the portal, waved above her. A flash of light came from the wand, and the second demon disappears, a cloud of dust drifting to the land below.

I didn't know the wand would do that, Annalome thought. Harrana could feel her astonishment.

Neither did I, their minds both heard in Meekian's voice. *Use it,* he demanded.

They did. Between the fire of all three dragons, arrows from the bows of Greg and Celia, and lethal light of Annalome's wand, they made short work of the remaining winged demon vanguard. Harrana, as wing leader, had a major decision to make: to fly for the portal or face the body of the winged demons nearly upon both the dragons and the allied army below. The choice was easy. The portal was a feint, a distraction. The winged demons were a real and imminent threat to the army. Harrana changed direction, her wingmen following her lead. She felt more than saw the unmounted dragons, five in total, join their formation. She knew none of them personally, and she was glad.

Her heart felt a great burden, a certainty that she now led those most dear to her to certain death.

She'd forgotten about the angels. *How did I forget the angels?*

I did too, Annalome answered.

᠅᠅᠅᠅᠅

Meekian flew low, intentionally staying within the range of the protective archers below. His heart longed to join the flight of dragons, but he bore the responsibility of command. Harrana and Annalome must watch the skies, making the immediate decisions for the wing of dragons. Meekian and Arthur must watch all, directing the flow of the entire battle, delaying tactic or not. Even with the patience of deep wisdom, the ancient dragon was frustrated knowing that the outcome of the day would be decided by an unknown element, and they all rested their hopes on faith in the contaminating presence of human goodness as it had touched demon lives over centuries.

The army holds well, Arthur thought to Meekian as they watched the land army below. They had been momentarily fearful when they saw the indigenous cavalry moving as though starting a spontaneous charge, one that would have been disastrous to the overall battle plan. The dragon and rider shared an internal sigh of relief when they saw the young Apache whom they had entrusted with command effectively hold his warriors, keeping their spontaneity in check. Instead, they watched as the pre-battle plans became reality below. Cavalry, infantry, and archers moved into planned positions like watching players on a board. While the army of demons milled and broiled with no organized ranks, the reptilians were as precise as well-oiled machinery. They formed three separate, double-rank lines all along the battle front, and the two contingents of cavalry, although not as precise, still moved easily to their assigned positions along the flanks. Even the hodgepodge infantry moved exactly as planned. Comprised primarily of human veterans of various ages and different armies, they were armed with rifles of all sorts, each one tipped with deadly bayonets. They were equipped also with modern plexiglass riot shields, a tool that had determined their primary purpose in this battle. They moved quickly to pair with archers, each infantryman positioned to use their shields to protect archers from the arrows of their counterparts among the demons.

Despite the frightening number of enemy forces, for the moment the land battle looked promising. That would change.

☙ ☙ ☙ ☙

Admiral O'Hare wished desperately he were on the deck of a ship. Holding an M-16 mounted with a well-sharpened bayonet and awkwardly maneuvering a full-length riot shield, he felt nearly useless. His old friend, Senior Chief Franconi, served as his second in command, but neither had access to the powerful weapons of the warships on which they had both served. O'Hare realized he and his command were little more than beasts of burden for the shields needed to protect the vital archers. He knew that if the battle came to him, if his bayonet became bloodied, there would be little hope for any of them.

Hopefully, he was wrong.

꧁꧂

When the attack began, the lines held. Stacks of demon bodies formed before the first line of reptilians, and demon arrows were useless against the two rank shield walls of the infantry, with the front rank impenetrable from the front and the second rank protecting from above. The cavalry was highly effective in picking off straggling groups. Their mobility also proved effective in avoiding the flights of arrows, thanks to the delay of delivery from those demon archers firing from back ranks.

But there were untold thousands of demons. They overcame the first rank of infantry not from superior fighting but by climbing the bodies of their own until the allied rank was buried in carnage, no longer effective, and it continued to the second rank. In a fairly short time, a few demons passed the infantry and O'Hare's bayonet was bloodied.

Arthur blew the war horn again and Meekian hoovered, deciding whether to join the fight below or the one in the air. There was still an open area, a front in the battle lines, but it was now facing the final rank of reptilians.

꧁꧂

From the clouds above, the angels descended upon the huge flight of winged demons like locusts on a field of wheat. The angels fought with swords and shields of light, and mini bolts of lightning more effective than any arrow. If a demon struck a deadly blow, the angel simply disappeared in a flash of light, but the demons had a more ignoble end. They fell like stones onto their own army, often crushing their comrades to death. The progress of the demons was nearly halted and only a handful made it through the lines, with all of those now flying toward Harrana and her wing of dragons. She realized their goal remained to stop Annalome and the wand she bore. Harrana changed direction, returning to their original mission. The entire wing—Maolan, Masat, and the unmounted dragons—followed her lead.

They met the contingent of winged demons within moments. There were at least thirty, just a fraction of the original force, but still a daunting obstacle for the eight dragons and three riders. The unmounted ones did well initially, incinerating six of the demons with their fire. Harrana saw when one dragon produced only smoke, it received a spear thrust between the scales of its natural armor and it plunged to the ground, already dead.

Away with you, Harrana commanded to the remaining four. *Replenish your fire to fight again.*

Obediently, the four banked sharply back to the rear of the allied army. A stockpile of sulfur stone awaited them there.

Harrana incinerated two more demons before she produced only smoke, but Annalome's effectiveness with the wand did not abate. Maolan and Masat had similar success with Greg and Celia making great use of an extensive supply of arrows. The force of demons was cut in half and they now withdrew, almost too abruptly for Harrana's comfort. They acted in unison, apparently responding to an order. Retreat was not a customary demon tactic. As they left, a demon just below Harrana loosed a parting arrow, and Harrana felt a sharp pain just above her tail. Annoying, but it did not affect her flight.

Although concerned at the demons' behavior, Harrana returned to her flight path toward the portal, now less than a half mile above her. That's when she heard the sound, a twang like an arrow leaving bow, but deeper and louder. She glanced toward the sound and saw a huge wooden bolt, sharpened and tipped in metal, heading directly toward her. She moved to bank away from the projectile but felt a firm grasp on her back, right behind the saddle. Coming from the rear, she had not seen the approach of the two winged demons who now held her in place. Below, she saw the Governor on his wooden platform, uncovered beside him was a massive crossbow, and he was reloading. Harrana inhaled, awaiting the strike of the bolt.

Maolan was there, almost by magic, placing herself between Harrana and the weapon. Harrana and Annalome screamed in agony as they watched the bolt strike Maolan. The green dragon made no sound as the bolt pierced her full center. The metal tip of the bolt narrowly missed Greg as it erupted from the dragon's back. With an effort Harrana couldn't even imagine, Maolan spread her wings, striving to glide to the ground, protecting her rider with all her strength.

Annalome pivoted in the saddle, using the wand to evaporate into dust the two demons that held them. Freed of their grasp, Harrana plunged toward Maolan while Masat and Celia did the same. As she flew, Harrana looked to the Governor and his crossbow, the shaft pointed at her again. She felt at peace, ready to die along with her friend, her lover, Maolan.

The Governor's savage smile enraged her, but it disappeared as the pointed end of a sword protruded out the front of his throat, his hand stilled from firing the crossbow. As he fell, Harrana glimpsed the Governess behind him, her hand on the hilt of the sword that had killed him.

The threat below was forgotten as they plunged, reaching the injured dragon in a flash. With hands and feet extended, both Harrana and Masat grasped Maolan's saddle, tail, legs, whatever they could hold to slow the injured dragon's fall. Greg pulled the quick release of the straps that held him to the saddle, and Annalome grasped his hand, pulling him to a seat behind her. They were effective but not totally. As a unit, they hit the ground with a thump, Greg knocked to the ground without straps to secure him to the saddle. For the first time, Maolan moaned as the shaft of the bolt hit the ground, forcing it even deeper through her body. Slightly winded, Harrana fought for breath as she looked up to realize they were amidst the front-line fighting, with mounted allies and infantry moving into position to protect the dragons.

Both Harrana and Masat had taken the brunt of hitting the ground. The dragons were stunned, and a force of demons broke the lines to rush in for the kill. It was the riders who saved them, the riders and remnants of the reptilian infantry. Annalome, Greg, and Celia fought like demons themselves to protect the fallen dragons. Shockingly, Celia showed a skill and passion beyond her comrades. She didn't even pause or take notice when a sword created a shallow slice that breached the light armor across her chest. She killed that demon with a single thrust, dispatching another before for the first had time to realize he was done.

From the front ranks of the enemy, a woman ran.

It was the dark-haired beauty Kidwell knew to be the true human self of the Governess. As she ran, an arrow found its way to her back. A squatty demon caught her as she fell, and his scream of pain overshadowed the cacophony of battle.

Pug, Harrana thought, recognizing the Governess's devoted servant. He gently laid the woman on the ground, then stood alone facing the demon army. As he did so, a small contingent of his own ilk joined him, forming a circle around the fallen woman. They looked so tiny against the massive dark warriors before them.

"You cannot have her," he called, his voice as strong and passionate as any Harrana had ever heard or even imagined.

The miracle happened.

Harrana and her comrades had seen earlier the blue aura surrounding the prayer warriors in the distance, safely unseen by the demon army. That aura filled the entire sky. For that matter, it filled the hearts of all present, and the entire demon force transformed into a black mist, sucked up into the portal like water down a toilet. Mixed with that blackness were wisps of blue, the blue trailing from the circle of demons who had surrounded the woman. When the entire cloud disappeared into the portal, the black hole snapped shut. What remained was blue sky with a scattering of wispy clouds.

The demon army was gone, although armor, weapons, and engines of war were scattered across the plain like toys abandoned on a playroom floor. Only one demon remained, sort of. A small dog lay half on the fallen, dark-haired woman. He whined and licked at the arrow protruding from the woman's back.

Once Harrana realized the battle was won, she turned her attention to all that mattered to her in that moment. Maolan, the dragon, was gone. Before her, Maolan the woman lay wounded and broken on the ground. Annalome knelt beside her, hands grasping at the entrance and exit wounds of the bolt. By some miracle, the huge bolt was now a simple arrow, proportional in size to Maolan's decrease in mass from dragon to human. Annalome wept, fighting a losing battle to stem the blood flow. Harrana transformed into Kidwell. She stood and felt a sharp pain in her left buttock. She reached to grasp and pull the arrow she'd taken in the battle, now just a tiny bolt, decreased proportionally in size as she'd transformed herself. Kidwell didn't even notice the pain of the extraction as she rushed to Maolan's side. She tore off her shirt, exposing the sports bra beneath, then wrapped the shirt hastily around Annalome's hands and the bleeding wounds.

"Hang on, Love," Kidwell said. "The healers will come."

As though in response to her wish, Aisha knelt beside them, her jar of healing ointment in her hands. Kidwell did not know what magic brought the prayer warriors so suddenly, but she thanked God for that magic. She glanced around the field of battle and saw other healers, including the bearded man in the rough-spun robe, White Buffalo Calf Woman, Meekian, and others she did not know. Aisha scooped ointment from the jar and prepared to touch it to Maolan's wounds. Maolan grasped Aisha's wrist.

"No," Maolan said.

"What?"

Maolan coughed slightly. She wiped at her mouth

with the back of her hand, and Kidwell saw a streak of blood on Maolan's hand and across her cheek.

"Too long I have lived without my Falong. It is time to cross the veil," Maolan said.

Kidwell wept so hard her chest ached. "Maolan, I—"

"If you love me, let me go," the Celt responded.

Annalome took her hands from the wounds, leaning over the dying woman. "Do you still hate me?" she asked.

Maolan touched Annalome's cheek, leaving a hint of bloody fingerprints. "My Annalome." She cocked her head to one side, a hint of revelation on her face. "I don't think I ever hated you, but I had to fight so hard not to love you." Her gaze went back and forth between the two women. "I love you both, and my Falong, but I long for him and always have. We were The Four. We will wait for you, dears, Falong and I. We will wait." She smiled as her breath rattled. Kidwell watched as Maolan's eyes went blank, without the spark of life.

Kidwell and Annalome held the body between them. They held each other, and they grieved. Tears were not enough. Kidwell's fist clenched so tight that her nails bit into her palm, and her blood joined that of Maolan's. They each wept not just with their eyes and bodies but with their very souls. Greg stood guard over his friends as Aisha joined the other healers on the field. Many were healed, but some were not. It was simply their time, as Meekian told the other healers when they expressed distress at their failures. One failure was a dark-haired beauty, one guarded by a tenacious little dog.

After a time, it was Greg who drew the task of

taking Kidwell from her grief. He grasped her shoulders, pulling her away from Annalome and Maolan.

"Kid, we need you."

Kidwell shook her head. Like it or not, she was a leader of this movement. No wound of body, heart, or soul could relieve her of that duty.

"What is it?"

"The dark-haired woman. She's dying, and she insists on talking with you," he answered. As he did so, he handed a water flask to Kidwell. "Drink this. It has a little of Aisha's ointment in it. It will give you strength."

Kidwell took the flask and drank deeply. She felt a flicker of will to live return. She knelt beside Annalome, placed the flask to the other woman's lips, and forced her to drink. She watched Annalome's face but saw only the blankness of grief.

"I have to go for a while," she told Annalome. The other woman's gaze lifted, and she nodded a reluctant understanding.

Greg led the way, Kidwell limping behind him, once again remembering the arrow she'd taken in the battle. She said nothing. Celia sat beside the dark-haired woman, and the little dog whined softly, still lying half on the fallen woman. Someone had broken the parts of arrow that had protruded from her body, and cloth bandages were already soaked in blood. Her lower half and one arm were covered with a cloak, one Kidwell recognized as Celia's.

"I was watching over her," Celia explained as Kidwell approached. "She had no friends."

Kidwell knelt and petted the small dog, who looked at her with such longing that it broke another piece of Kidwell's heart that she could not save his mistress.

"You were right," the woman said, her eyes still closed. Kidwell had thought her unconscious.

"Right about what?"

"As long as there is life, there is hope of changing our choices."

"You most certainly did, and we are all grateful," Kidwell responded.

The woman's hand shook as she reached up to pet the dog. "Can you please care for my loyal Pug? It would seem I cannot."

Kidwell sat on the ground beside the woman and the dog, wincing slightly as her injured hip touched the ground.

"Of course I'll care for him. He saved us all, you know."

"I wondered what happened. How did he save us?"

"All we needed was one act of love from the enemy. That was all required to complete the bridge of love being created by the Matrix, the prayer warriors."

"I see," the woman said.

"I'm sorry our healers could not help you."

"I'm not. I've lived too long and have too much to atone for." She started to take a deep breath but instead shuddered in pain. "Let me go in peace, riding on the glory of my one courageous act. I'm tired now. Leave me."

Kidwell shook her head at the command in the dying woman's voice. Old habits were hard to break. She stood awkwardly, favoring her hip.

"You'll stay with her?" she asked Celia.

"Sure. No one should die alone. Besides, I'm reminded that living a selfish life leads to a lonely end."

Kidwell nodded, trying to muster a smile in her dirt- and tear-caked face. She wondered where the anger and the betrayal had gone that she'd once felt so strongly toward this woman. Greg was at her side again. She hadn't realized he'd stayed so close. As he approached her, he leaned over, studying her ass closely, noticing the streak of blood from her butt and forming a line down her pant leg.

"Whatcha looking at?"

"You're wounded."

"No shit."

"Aisha needs to see to that,"

"When she has time."

"Besides…" He raised one eyebrow as he looked around her to see the blood on her pants. "I thought you were *facing* the enemy."

In the midst of the grief and the pain and the devastation, it started with a giggle for all three of them—Greg, Kidwell, and Celia—and grew to a laugh so hysterical they each fell to the ground and little Pug barked a warning not to disturb his mistress. It ended in uncontrollable tears and the realization that the dark-haired woman was dead.

Chapter Twenty

A Brand-New Day

Bob stirred his coffee absently, a fruitless effort considering he had also forgotten to imbue that coffee with his usual milk and sugar. His wife, sitting across from him at the kitchen table, seemed equally discombobulated. Both of them had sections of the morning paper spread out before them, searching for news. They read of the miracle, of the sudden and unexplained comas of both leaders whose childish tiff had threatened world annihilation, but that didn't feel "right" to Bob. He suspected something else had happened. Bob had no clue what it would be, but they were both certain something huge had happened in the night.

"We never oversleep," his wife said. She seemed to rouse from her stupor to notice her husband stirring black coffee. He didn't notice as she added a spoonful of sugar and a dollop of milk to the no longer dark liquid.

"And both of us? The dreams were so, well, weird," he responded, finally putting down the spoon and sipping at the coffee. A plate of cold toast sat between them, untouched.

"The same dreams," she said. "How did we have the same dreams?"

"When I called in to work, Mitsy said I wasn't

the only one out sick today. She said five people called in with some sort of sleep disturbance. They all overslept."

"I called Jean at the shop," his wife said. "No answer, so I called her at home. She'd overslept, and she said she had the wildest dreams."

"Tell me again what you dreamed," he said.

"Same as you. We were together, but there were thousands of us, and we were, well, praying, I guess. It was for something important. We were flying, all of us, in…no, not in. We were part of this huge blue cloud."

"And it worked!"

"I know! I woke up feeling the most incredible joy."

They both turned to stare toward the dining room as they heard a distinct *clop-clop* of horse's hooves on the wooden floor. A unicorn stepped into the archway between the two rooms. Mounted on him was their son, Tommy, wearing light leather armor and a steel helmet. The couple sat gaping at the sight.

"I was a messenger," Tommy announced proudly. "They wouldn't let me fight."

"He was very brave," the unicorn said.

Bob's coffee cup slipped from his hand and spilled coffee across the table.

Tommy slipped from the unicorn's back and headed for the paper towels on the kitchen counter, moving to clean up the spill his father was too shocked to notice.

"Pardon me," the unicorn added. "Would you happen to have any of those frosted corn flakes? I've grown quite fond of them."

Most of the army was gone, returned to their different worlds bearing the dead and aiding those wounded but not completely cured by the work of the healers. Only the dragons and the riders remained. There had been much debate as to what to do with the body of the dark-haired woman. No one knew her origins or what she would wish to call home. In the end, they had buried her there, in the liminal space between the worlds. A cairn of stones marked the grave, topped with the sword she'd used to dispatch the Governor. It seemed a proper memorial. They knew no name to put on a stone, so Harrana did what she could. Finding a flat rock and etching with dragon claws as strong as steel, she wrote: *A woman who lived to make a better choice.*

Maolan posed a different problem. She belonged to more than one world—dragon and human. In the end they gave her the traditional rite of a dragon rider. There could be no greater honor than cremation by dragon fire. After adding their flames to the pyre, the circle of dragons who loved her keened a mourning that could make the very earth weep. Once the fires burned, Harrana became Kidwell, and she and Annalome held each other as they voiced their own grief, so stricken they could not stand. Aisha, Greg, and Martin—still limping from an almost healed spear wound to his thigh—gathered around the two women, supporting them and weeping their own grief.

She was the greatest of riders and the greatest of dragons, Meekian thought to all, offering a simple eulogy. Her ashes would go to both worlds, and those who loved her would be given the opportunity to say goodbye. Masat would take them to the weyr and valley where Maolan had lived for so very long. Kidwell would take them to the Irish village, the home she'd shared with Maolan for too short a time.

Only Meekian, Kidwell, and Annalome remained on the battlefield. Greg and Aisha had returned to their home in Texas, ready to repair what damage the demons had done. In this liminal space, they didn't even need a painting portal for the journey, they needed only jointly envision the home they shared. Celia showed more fear at her return home than she had before, during, or after the battle.

"Your mother will see you changed, Celia," Annalome said. "Your brothers will come around, in time."

To her own surprise, Kidwell put an arm around Celia's shoulders. "You have found your courage, woman. It won't fail you now."

Fearful as she was, Celia took a deep breath, closed her eyes, and then she was gone, back to *la familia de ella*. Martin returned to the *ranchito* in New Mexico, the brindle-colored dog snuggled in his arms. The dark-haired woman had been duly mourned, for the little dog had to be forcefully carried from her grave. He had howled pitifully until Kidwell held him close, looking into his dark eyes.

"It was her last wish that we care for you," she said. "Would you have us disappoint her?"

The little dog seemed to understand, and he grew silent, but tears still streamed from his eyes. Kidwell had never seen a dog cry like that before.

Now, the three stood alone: Meekian, Kidwell, and Annalome. They walked in silence, feeling too profoundly the recent events to have any need for conversation.

Fly with me, Meekian thought. Kidwell transformed to Harrana and Annalome climbed into the saddle, tightening the straps to hold her in place. They flew in a wide circle above the battleground, still cluttered with the abandoned armor and weapons of the demons. Harrana was surprised as they flew over an arroyo to see that a spring had begun to flow, putting water into a long, dry creek bed. She suspected this desert would bloom again now that the battle was won. Meekian led them back to the site of the healers, the prayer circle. As they drew closer the sweet scent of magic still hung in the air. From the sky above, Harrana thought she recognized White Buffalo Calf Woman's handiwork, for a large stone medicine wheel marked the place where they had prayed and worked their magic. Meekian landed gently beside the wheel, with Harrana and Annalome landing nearby. He turned to face the dragon-rider pair.

It is time, he thought.

Time? Harrana asked.

Yes, time for me to cross the veil.

No! Why? Harrana and Annalome both demanded. *You survived the battle,* Harrana added.

It is my choice, child. Maolan longed for her dragon, and I long for my rider. Arthur was called home as soon as the battle was won. Our brief time reunited only increased the ache I've known for most of my existence.

But we need you, Harrana thought.

The dragon and human world may need a representative of the most ancient of dragons, but I have an heir now. I can go where I long to be.

Me? Harrana answered, a hint of bitterness in the

thought.

Yes.

I'm not ready.

If you thought you were, I would not dare leave. A secret of wisdom is that it is never fully attained. Strive for it always.

Harrana huffed, tendrils of smoke escaping from each nostril. Annalome reached beyond the saddle, resting a hand on her dragon's shoulder.

Harrana, my love. When we were apart, remember the pain?

Harrana's head bowed, her nose nearly touching the ground. *I am frightened of what you ask of me.* She looked Meekian in the eye. *I am lost at the thought of a world without you.* She took a deep breath and raised her head high. *But I understand what you must do. We love you, Meekian, and we will miss you.*

The most ancient of all living dragons touched his forehead to Harrana's, then moved to gently do the same to the much smaller Annalome.

Be well, dragon and rider. Lead as best you can. No one could do more.

Perhaps at his bidding, a ring of light appeared above the medicine wheel. Meekian sprung into the air and into the light, which immediately flashed to darkness. He was gone.

Chapter Twenty-one

Homes Sweet Homes

Kidwell awoke, feeling the warmth of a well-loved woman spooning behind her. For a disconcerting moment, she couldn't remember which of two women lay beside her. In the next instant, waking memory flooded her mind and heart. The waves of joy and pain were so intense that she had to remind herself to breathe.

In the months since the battle, she and Anna had returned to their old life as much as possible, but now they had two homes. In New Mexico, they'd returned to the old routine of a life with Martin, their soul-son, including rides in the mountains, care for the horses and land, and the daily business of a modern Prophet and her partner, aided by Admiral O'Hare who bore the brunt of the business end. Even Celia had returned to her apartment over the barn, although the dynamic was far different than the former life. One other major change was the little dog, a gentle creature who had so bonded with Martin that they were never apart. Even when the four humans took the horses into the woods or along the valleys, the little pug trotted happily beside Martin's paint gelding or, when tired, rode in front of his new master, draped across the swells of the saddle and watching the passing scenery contentedly.

Then there was their other home, one they had

visited only when essential during the weeks they claimed as a healing time. Meekian's cave was now Harrana's cave, but she was not doomed to the solitude that had been Meekian's plight. Her adopted sister and niece had left their weyr to live in the complex cave, for there was much to do, more than any one dragon and rider could accomplish alone. Even Celia divided her time between the worlds, helping in the labors.

After Meekian's passing, Harrana and Annalome postponed their return to the human world. Harrana knew she could not delay accepting the mantle of responsibility the ancient dragon had placed upon her shoulders. There, they had found all that Meekian had promised—or warned. Harrana wasn't sure which it was, or perhaps both. She alone visited the reflective pool hidden deep within the cave. There was ancient magic there, and even the cave complied; where she found a passage, the others saw only a stone wall. Harrana touched the pool tentatively with her snout, and she felt and heard a tentative message: *Welcome.*

I am here, her mind heard. It was Meekian's voice. *I am well and happy.* There was a murmur of a thousand voices behind him, then it went silent. At that moment it was simply a peaceful pool, lit by an unexplained light that exuded from the stone itself. Harrana left. She would return when needed.

The second discovery Meekian promised proved a shock that sent Harrana collapsing on her backside, tendrils of smoke exuding from each nostril. Annalome was so surprised she leaned against her dragon for support. The chamber was not hard to find; Meekian had walked it so many times over the millennia that a deep path was worn in the stone. As they drew close, a light grew, the same magical glow Harrana has seen in the pool chamber. Inside, there was a clutch of fifteen eggs—dragon eggs—and from the bright color of the scales that covered them, Harrana knew they were of her kin, her species, the most ancient of all dragonkind.

They wasted no time, using the portals between worlds to shortcut the long flight to the weyr where Masat lived. Harrana had no experience caring for a clutch of eggs, especially ones that had lain dormant for untold centuries. So it was that Masat, with Allana as her willing apprentice, became nursemaid to a dragon dream come true. Using their fire, Masat and Allana heated the bed of stone beneath the eggs. After hearing of the miracle of the eggs, Celia begged to join in their care. When first heated, her human body could not bear the temperature of the chamber, but she returned when they cooled somewhat, wearing a special suit she made of leather over a layer of cool padding. She would join the two dragon nursemaids in turning the eggs, something that had to be done at least five times during the course of a day. Celia used the portal—a painting Aisha created of the interior of the barn at Kidwell and Anna's *ranchito*—to travel between her care for horses and her care for dragon eggs.

Kidwell thought of all these things as she lay enjoying the warmth of her bed and her woman. She heard the rhythm of Anna's breathing change, and she knew her lover, her dragon rider, was awake.

"I don't want to move," Kidwell said.

"Then don't," Anna mumbled against her neck.

"Masat said the baby dragons have begun to move inside the eggs."

Anna sat up, her sleepiness forgotten and replaced by excitement. "When? When did she say that?"

"When I checked with her through the portal

last night. You were already asleep."

Anna threw back the covers and swatted Kidwell soundly on the ass. "Get up then. We've got things to do."

"Ouch!"

Anna grinned at her slyly over her shoulder as she walked toward the bathroom. "But you like to be spanked."

Kidwell enjoyed viewing the hint of round buttocks she could see just below the hem of Anna's nightshirt. "In the right circumstances, yes, I do."

Anna turned in the doorway and placed a hand on each hip in a gesture of impatience. "Well then if you hurry and get dressed, maybe we'll have time for different 'circumstances' later today."

It was then they heard a distinctive *thump-thump* from the stairs leading to their upstairs bedroom. A brindle-colored pug appeared at the top of the stairs, giving them two impatient barks. Kidwell took a deep breath, enjoying the smell of brewing coffee.

"Smells like Martin is fixing breakfast."

Anna laughed and pointed at the dog. "He's obviously here, otherwise our little friend wouldn't have been sent for our wake-up call." She turned back into the bathroom, closing the door behind her with a snap.

"Well, guess I'm using the downstairs bathroom," Kidwell mumbled to herself. She rose and dressed, using the jeans she'd left on the chair beside the bed and a fresh T-shirt from her dresser drawer. By the time she'd washed her face and brushed her teeth in the downstairs bathroom, Martin was calling loudly from the kitchen, telling the two women that breakfast was ready. Anna's hair was still wet from her quick shower when she took her seat at the table. As they ate the *chorizo* and scrambled eggs, rolled in freshly heated flour tortillas, Kidwell told Martin the news about the dragon eggs.

"That's fantastic," Martin said as he slipped a piece of tortilla to the dog sitting patiently by his chair.

"Want to come with us?" Kidwell asked.

"We're getting a load of hay this morning," Martin answered. "Will you take me later?"

Kidwell nodded. "By then, you may have the chance to meet some new baby dragons."

As they talked, Anna looked at the little dog beside Martin's chair. "Do you think he remembers being a demon?" she asked.

"Talking about me or the dog?" Martin responded.

"Hardy, har, har," Anna said.

"Thought maybe you knew something I didn't."

"I think he remembers loving the dark-haired woman," Kidwell said.

"A love that saved us all," Anna added.

Martin chewed slowly, then swallowed before answering. "I don't think he ever had the heart of a demon."

Kidwell considered his comment. "You may be right, which makes me wonder about the nature of demons."

"Or the nature of all existence," Anna said. "How does good and evil really fit in the big picture?"

"Maybe good and evil *is* the big picture," Kidwell responded.

Martin groaned. "Oh, God. I can't handle existential philosophy on only one cup of coffee." The women laughed. "Besides, I don't wonder so much about what Pug was as I do about what he will be."

"What do you mean?" Kidwell asked.

"You know, in his next life." Martin looked at the small dog, clearly touched by the devotion he saw in the animal's eyes. "He'll be a person, a man, I think. I feel certain of that."

"Maybe he and the dark-haired woman aren't done yet," Anna added.

Kidwell reached across the table to take her lover's hand. "Thank God we weren't. Done, that is."

Anna laid her fork on her plate and grasped Kidwell's hand in both her own. "Yes, thank God."

Martin groaned again. "Oh man, philosophy and true love." He rose from the table, cup in hand. "I need more coffee."

They left the unwashed dishes in the sink, Kidwell admonishing Martin to leave them for later, stating that he'd cooked so they'd clean. Anna retrieved her boots from the service porch and headed up the stairs. Kidwell didn't bother with boots. Once they were through the portal she'd be dragon, and boots weren't needed. By the time she reached the top of the stairs, Anna had her boots on and was standing beside the dragon-eye painting.

"Let's go," Anna said impatiently.

Kidwell laughed, then took her lover's hand. Together they took the fluid form that had become so familiar, and they appeared on the other side. They stood beside the dragon-eye portal Allana had moved from their family weyr to Meekian's cave. No one greeted them, and with Harrana leading the way they made their way directly down the path to the egg cave. There they found Masat, Allana, and Celia anxiously hovering over the clutch of eggs. The two dragons were using fire incrementally, keeping the stones warm without making the cavern unbearably hot for the humans. Celia sat near the nest of stones, her gloved hand resting on a bright red egg that rocked and wiggled beneath her hand. Harrana saw the sweat streaming down Celia's face and wished she'd thought to bring jugs of ice water for the two women. She did note the water jug resting behind Celia but wondered how near it must be to empty.

Finally, you're here, Masat thought to her sister.

We knew you had everything under control, Harrana answered.

As though on cue, timed for their arrival, the egg Celia nursed so carefully cracked. The nose of a small dragon could be seen pushing to break through the membrane below the scaled shell. Celia reached with a gloved hand and gently tore at the membrane. As soon as it was breached, the hatchling gave a mighty push and the shell broke away in a multitude of sections. Celia reached out to steady the unstable hatchling, and as she touched the young female dragon, a wave of light and a musical tone, loud but pleasant, filled the cavern.

The three adult dragons roared in joy, and Anna laughed in ecstasy, remembering when she and Harrana had shared such a moment.

Celia gasped, shocked and pleased and totally confused. "What just happened?" she demanded.

You're a rider, Celia. A rider! Harrana thought to all present.

"You and your dragon are the first to bond in millennia," Anna called, laughing.

Another egg, a green one, began to rock precariously. The entire cavern filled with something brighter than any light. Hope lived. Hope for humanity and dragonkind unlike.

In the midst of that hope, Harrana had a thought that she kept only to herself. *Could there be Four? Could there be Four again?*

Epilogue

Peace at Last

It was the weyr as she remembered it. Below were the thatched roofs of the village where she was born, not the modern Irish town where she and Kidwell had lived. Maolan sat on the stone ledge, enjoying the sunshine and never forgotten scent of Ireland before there was even an Ireland. There was a sense of peace unlike any she had ever known. It wasn't just the breeze and the clouds. It went beyond her physical senses and filled her heart, her very soul.

"Welcome home," a voice said from the cave behind her.

Maolan turned to see a tall, handsome man approach her. He took a cross-legged seat on the stone shelf beside her, so close he was nearly touching. She looked into the depth of eyes so blue they were...no, not blue. They were purple, the color of her dragon, of—

"Falong," she whispered. She should have felt shock, even surprise, but those emotions seemed absent. Instead, there was deep peace.

"You told Kidwell you envied her having experienced the love of her rider as both a dragon and a human," the man said.

Maolan simply moved closer, accepting the arm he placed around her shoulders and laying her head on his shoulder.

"You heard what I said to Kidwell?" she asked.

"Of course. I never stopped watching you, waiting for you."

"Harrana? Annalome? Will they—"

"In time, when it is right, they will join us," Falong answered. "They still have work to do."

They both looked at the sky as they heard the telltale swish of a dragon in flight just as a red dragon, an Eastern dragon, completed a circle toward the stone shelf and landed neatly beside them. A youth leapt from the saddle, laughing as he did so.

"Isn't it a grand thing, Maolan?" the youth asked. "Being with our dragons again?"

There should have been confusion, as both dragon and rider were so young they were barely beyond child and fledgling, but she knew them.

"Meekian, Arthur! It is so good to see you," she said, rising to touch foreheads with the dragon and embrace the youth in a warm hug. She looked around, and for an instant felt a hint of confusion. "Where exactly are we?" she asked.

Beyond the veil, dear greatest of riders and greatest of dragons, she heard Meekian say in her mind.

The youth leapt back into the saddle, tightening the straps across his thighs and waist to hold him in place. "Let's fly," he called. "There is so much to show you."

"For that to happen," Falong the man, said. *I must change,* Falong the dragon, thought.

Laughing as gleefully as the youth, Maolan leapt to her own saddle, and the straps were barely snug as the four of them took to the air.

They flew. Maolan experienced her first flight that had absolutely no boundaries.

If you liked this book?

Reviews help a new author get discovered and if you have enjoyed this book, please do the author the honor of posting a review on Goodreads, Amazon, Barnes & Noble or anywhere you purchased the book. Or perhaps share a posting on your social media sites or spread the word to your friends.

About the Author

As a writer and consultant Kayt C. Peck has worked with many diverse organizations over the years. She has found wisdom in the words and lives of people of all colors, religious beliefs, sexual orientations, gender identities, nationalities, and socioeconomic classes. Her multicultural exposure heavily influenced the writing of this magical realism series starting with The Kiva and the Mosque, then The Pyramid and the Painting, and finally, The Past and the Present. Her lifelong career as a writer has included working as a journalist, a public affairs officer in the US Naval Reserve, and as a grant expert, writing applications raising more than $30 million for worthy domestic and even international organizations. She has published several novels, one biography, and written many plays. As a playwright, she is a two-time awardee in the Rocky Mountain Voices play competition and received a special award, "Excellence in Play Writing," at the American Association of Community Theatre's Region VI 2015 finals. She has authored and published numerous articles, short stories, and poems. The first edition of The Kiva and the Mosque and her novel Good Water were both finalists in the New Mexico/ Arizona Book Awards. Today, she lives quietly in her cabin home in the mountains of northeastern New Mexico.

Other books by Kayt

Good Water- ISBN- 978-1-939062-87-1

The dry plains drew Judy Proctor like a bear to her den...or a moth to the flame. Ranching was her life. The sweat as she branded or "doctored" cattle...the howl of a coyote in the quiet, night air...half-frozen fingers as she cut the wire to loosen hay bales for hungry cattle scratching for survival in snow-covered land...all of the everyday existence on the ranch was her life. It was where she belonged. It was a lonely life.

She had tried to leave the ranch to join the "normal" existence of a talented young woman in the city, but it had never been home. When her parents were killed in an automobile accident, she returned to the family ranch as much because she needed it as it needed her. She faced a lonely life to be shared with no better company than Somegood and Useless, her cow dog and the mottled mutt that were her companions.

Kathleen Romero slipped into Judy's life unexpectedly. She came to the plains to write a story. Would she stay because of the real truth she found in the simple drama of husbanding land and animals?

Unfortunately, even wide-open spaces can be plagued by prejudice and closed-minds. As the two women struggle to know each other, they must also carve a place for themselves among the country-folk who have been Judy's friends and neighbors her entire life.

The Ladies Room - ISBN - 978-1-943353-09-3

A dream is housed in the dusty, unused storage room above the Pink Triangle, one of Amber, Texas' two gay bars. Journalist April Sims serves as the reluctant leader in making that dream a reality. Under her guidance an eclectic group of women build a safe place in a community where being a lesbian can be dangerous and difficult.

April meets Sophia Mendez, a local attorney, as she seeks legal guidance for members of the group. In meeting with the women of the Ladies' Room, Sophia finds herself dealing with personal as well as professional issues.

When a radical religious group levels an attack on the entire gay community, even to the the point of a vigilante attack on the Pink Triangle, the strength and unity of the women of The Ladies' Room will be tested to the core.

Only time will tell if the beauty of the dream can override the ugliness of a harsh reality.

Prairie Fire - ISBN – 978-1-943353-47-7

Judy and Kathleen were accepted, even loved, by their conservative ranching neighbors. Their world felt safe and secure...until...until prairie fire! The flames disrupted their lives, causing destruction and injury, but the community pulled together to face a common enemy. When Kathleen's unofficial "daughter" found herself homeless, Pookie joined that community, bringing to this simple world her black clothes and rebellious nature. Together, conservative and liberal, gay and straight, they were a community, ready to face fire itself. The surprise to them all was the unseen enemy from within, one that had the potential to destroy them all.

The Kiva and The Mosque - ISBN - 978-1-943353-85-9

In a troubled world, answers rarely come from where they are expected. The need for answers to save a troubled humanity forces Kidwell Brown and Aisha Sudda, two total strangers, into roles they never could have anticipated. Kidwell and her life-partner, Anna Montoya, live a quiet life in their mountain home until the day Kidwell is drawn to visit the ceremonial cave at Bandelier National Monument. Hundreds of miles away, Aisha Sudda Fletcher lives another quiet existence, along with her husband, Greg, until the day she is drawn to visit a garden beside a vandalized mosque.

On that day, both Kidwell and Aisha are chosen. These humble women soon learn that the time of prophets has not yet passed. During mystical moments, each woman is given a message – "Desert Lightning has no power" to Kidwell, and "The scimitar has no edge," to Aisha. They each pass along the message as instructed, neither realizing they have predicted important moments in world history.

Their mystical guides direct the women to "find their allies," and so the lives of Kidwell, Aisha, Anna and Greg are forever intertwined. They will face victory and exile, mystery and certainty.

In the end the very nature of humanity proves to be the world in which they must fight and survive.

As an unabashed advocate for the gay/lesbian/ bisexual/transgendered community in places were being different was dangerous, Kayt honed her skill in standing her ground and doing the right thing. Her entertaining and thought-provoking novels offer readers a rich banquet of characters, settings and scenarios that leave us both satisfied and wanting more.

Best-selling author Anne Hillerman

The Pyramid and the Painting - ISBN - 978-1-948232-13-5

Great magic comes with great gifts and great burdens. Kidwell and Anna must face together the ramifications of being thrust into world-changing roles. such responsibility exacts a price in their own lives and the many lifetimes they've shared before. The magic Kidwell and her co-prophet, Aisha, stumbled into in the first book in the series, Kiva and the Mosque, continues to push them all into situations they never could have imagined. As their life-partners, Kidwell's Anna and Aisha's Greg, must find their own strength and fight their own battles.

Not even great magic can prevent or cure a broken heart, but, sometimes, a broken heart is the only key to even deeper magic. Through great pain, Kidwell faces a transformation that has a profound effect not only on their lives but many lives across many worlds.

Other books by Sapphire Authors

Highland Dew – ISBN – 978-1-948232-11-1

Bryce Andrews, west coast sales director for Global Distillers and Distribution, is tired of the corporate hamster wheel. She needs a change.

A craft whisky trade show offers her inspiration and a chance to revisit Scotland and the majestic scenery of the Speyside region—best known for the "Whisky Trail." Bryce and her coworker, Reggie Ballard, need to find a wholly original whisky for their international distribution division by visiting a number of small distillers.

A blind curve, a dangling sign, and weed-choked driveway draw Bryce directly into a truly unique opportunity. She discovers a struggling family, a shuttered distillery, and a spitfire of a daughter called home to care for her confused father.

Fiona McDougall—the only child and heir to the MacDougall & Son legacy, had her career teaching in Edinburgh curtailed by fate…or serendipity.

When the stars finally align, the two women work together to resurrect a dream for themselves and the family business—if they can weather the storms of unscrupulous business practices in the competitive whisky market.

McCall - ISBN - 978-1-948232-32-6

Sara Brighton is a quickly rising culinary star in Savannah after Food & Wine magazine named her restaurant Best New Restaurant of the South, until it burns to the ground in an accident and she impulsively packs her truck and heads for McCall, Idaho, the last place she remembers being truly happy.

Sam Draper, head of the Lake Patrol division of the McCall PD, knows the last thing she needs is another entitled tourist making her life difficult on the water. However, after Sara surprises her by helping her avoid a near professional disaster, Sam teaches her to drive a boat. The chemistry between them is hot and instant, and as the summer heats up, Sam finds herself falling in love until Sara buys her late father's iconic diner and turns it into the newest hotspot for pretentious culinary tourists.

Can the love Sam and Sara found on the water survive the lingering ghosts waiting for them back on dry land?

Silver Love – ISBN – 978-1-948232-51-7

Jill, Dory, Robby, and Charlene are a fantastic foursome that embodies the varying experiences that come with being Lesbians of a Certain Age. They are vibrant and vulnerable, wise and foolish, introspective and outgoing. The close-knit friends fight aging at every turn—or just ignore it altogether. These four will never go quietly into the night, redefining life after fifty. They are the new mature woman.

But along with twenty-first-century attitudes come twenty-first-century problems. Public office candidate and retired judge Charlene is confronted by a wannabe blackmailer, Jill's passions threaten to swamp her common sense, Dory's best-selling book could turn out to be a national disaster, and Robby must confront the hard reality of learning that her wife may not be the woman she thought she was. Steadfast in their faith in themselves and each other, and bolstered by the rich history of their friendship, the four women struggle with twists and turns as they try to navigate a landscape generated by the actions of others as well as their own choices, proving that experience does not always pave a smooth road.

In a world where everything increasingly seems relative, these women remind us that some things don't change—like the bedrock of relationships. Silver Love is all about love; love among friends, love between lovers, and the unexpected role of love with acquaintances who may not always be what they seem.

If you can keep up, join the ride and follow these ageless heroines as they pursue their adventures in the modern world.

Twisted Deception - ISBN - 978-1-939062-47-5

There are two types of people who can't look you in the eyes: someone trying to hide a lie and someone trying to hide their love.

Addie Blake's life isn't black and white—more like a series of short bursts of color that sustain her until the next eruption. She isn't a ladder-climber in the corporate world. Instead, she works long hours at the office and even at home, something her mechanic girlfriend, Drake Hogan, can't stand. If Addie can't focus on Drake, then Drake finds arm candy that will. After a long week of late nights and a series of text-messaged demands, each one a bigger bomb than the last, Addie has had enough of her Motor Girl.

Greyson Hollister inhabits a world where everything is either black and white, or money green. She's a polished, certified workaholic. As head of Integrated Financial, she has built the ladder others want to climb. Now she intends to attend a business mixer to confront a rumormonger and kill merger rumors involving her company.

Detective Nancy Hill, the lead detective on the Elevator Rapist task force, has just been called in to investigate an attack at Integrated Financial. She can't quite put her finger on it, but something doesn't add up with this latest assault, and Greyson Hollister isn't exactly lending a helping hand.

A storm's brewing on the horizon. Can Addie and Greyson weather it, or will it blow them over?

Hearts INN – ISBN – 978-1-948232-36-4

Rosalie Campbell is bequeathed a rundown hotel in rural New Mexico in her grandmother's will. She arrives to discover a dried-out shell of a place that barely makes enough money to stay afloat. In a state of limbo with her girlfriend and accounting job in Philadelphia, Rosalie is keen to sell the hotel and go back to the comfort of her urban life. When new information about her grandmother surfaces and the hotel proves difficult to sell, Rosalie tries to attract buyers by restoring the building to its former glory with the help of Alex Ecker, a local handywoman. In the process, Rosalie learns a few things about hotel management, hard work, and opening her heart.

Blueprint for Romance: A Garriety Romance – ISBN – 978-1-948232-71-5

After the death of her husband, Dylan Lake's ability to trust in others is shattered. Her life is thrust into turmoil between caring for Emma, her seven-year old handicapped child, and working hard to make ends meet. Dylan doesn't have time to pursue a romantic relationship. Finding that one special person only happens in dreams. When fate keeps throwing Dylan and Kat together, Dylan finds her attraction to Kat something she can't ignore. Will her trust issues stop her from letting Kat into her and Emma's life? Leaving her old job and moving halfway across the country were the scariest things Kat Anderson had ever done. Starting a new life and career takes priority over any foolish notion of a fairy-tale future of romance and love. Kat's attraction to Dylan is time taken away from building a new business. Can Kat juggle love and duty to find her Happy Ever After? Welcome back to Garriety, the town with an open heart, and home to some of the quirky and warm characters from Add Romance and Mix. Join Kat and Dylan on their quest for true romance with a little help from Kat's sister Briley and her family, along with a host of new characters.